The Malevolent Twin

"The story of a wayward wicked twin
with destructive intentions"

Mary Sage Nguyen

ISBN: 978-0-9962561-0-0
ISBN-13: 978-0996256100

For my mother Muoi Tang Nguyen

ACKNOWLEGEMENTS

To my muse, Perry Faulk

To my editor, anonymous

To my book cover designers, the Ebook Launch team

You all have my eternal gratitude for assisting me with the creation of "The Malevolent Twin".

"Twins are usually hailed with delight,
because they swell the power of the family,
though in some instances they are put to death."

John Hanning Speke

Prologue

DR. MATTHEWS CARRIED THE NEWBORN BABY GIRL back to her parents. The surgery was successful. He looked down lovingly at the Asian infant dozing happily in his hands—she reminded him of his own daughter. Doctor Matthews had removed the majority of the baby's disfigurements. In the hospital room, her parents sat nervously waiting for the doctor.

"Hi Dr. Matthews. What is the news?" the father asked. He was a black-haired Vietnamese American and still dressed in his work clothes. His light blue shirt's logo read "Blue's Trucking" and there were grease stains all over his pants.

"Well, we were able to remove the extra limb."

"That is good news," the mother said, taking the baby from the doctor's arms. She had long hair—black, like her husband's—and brown eyes. She was sporting a big black bruise on her arm that her plum-colored dress didn't fully cover. The doctor didn't say anything about it. He knew it was not his place.

"I am really surprised we did not catch it earlier in the pregnancy."

"Well, I am just glad little Avery is okay," the father said in his broken English. He started to light a cigarette.

"Sir, really? In front of Avery?" the doctor asked him. Matthews did not approve of Mr. Tran. In fact the only reason he had performed the surgery was because the church gave him the cash for it. Also he had fallen in love with little Avery Tran as soon as met her. The Tran family was poor. Families similar to them typically could not afford Dr. Matthews' services. The Catholic church next door to the hospital had sponsored the surgery for Avery.

"You're right, I will do it outside," the father replied. He strolled out of the room.

"I'm glad my daughter is not going to be a freak and can live a normal life now," the mother said to the doctor. He stroked Avery's head softly.

"Yes, I believe she will," he replied.

Little Avery was still sleeping comfortably in her mother's arms. The evil and sinister presence inside of Avery's body boiled with anger. It was furious and ready for revenge.

Chapter One

The Arm

Avery Tran stood in front of her car on the side of the
highway. She opened the hood of her white 1992 two-door
Honda Accord. The engine was smoking and she coughed after
breathing in some of the fumes. She couldn't figure out what
going on with the engine since she had been driving smoothly.
She had forgotten her phone at home and the cars that whizzed
by offered no help. Avery was sweaty from the Texas heat,
even though she was wearing tiny shorts and a red tank top.

Her voluptuous figure caught the eye of an old man coast-
ing down the freeway. He pulled his blue BMW over and drove
up behind her Accord. He was balding but had enough hair to
tie into a grey ponytail. He wore a grey suit with a pink shirt
and his eyes were covered by a pair of thick black sunglasses.
This man couldn't keep his eyes off Avery. She was a wet
dream: a beautiful petite Asian woman with long silky black
hair. Her eyes were the color of chocolate diamonds and she
had nice supple legs perched on red high heels.

"Hey there. Are you having some car trouble?" the man
asked.

"Yes, I can't figure out what is going on with my car. And
I forgot my phone at home," Avery replied. The red tank top
hugged her stomach due to the sweat. Avery didn't know that
this man had stopped because of her appealing appearance. She
just thought he was being a kind stranger.

"I can take a look."

"Please do."

The man bent over the car's hood. He looked at the engine—it was a mess. Avery stood beside him watching him. The man didn't know a thing about cars but he pretended he knew just so he could impress Avery. The minutes dragged on and the man continued to fumble around with the car. Another car pulled up behind his, a red Mustang, driven by an old classmate of Avery's. She knew him fairly well. He had tousled brown hair and dreamy green eyes. His name was Nathan Belford. He was wearing blue jeans and a white polo shirt. You could see the outline of his impressive body through the white polo.

"Hey, it's Avery right?" Nathan said nervously. He hoped that was her name. He vaguely remembered her from high school. Back then she was skinny and wore glasses, but she had turned into a beautiful woman after all.

"Yeah, that's me."

"Do you need help with the car?" Nathan said strolling up to her.

"Two heads are better than one," Avery said with a smile. The man who had been trying to help Avery earlier scooted over for Nathan to see the engine.

"Oh I see what is going on. You are missing your oil cap." The man next to Nathan snorted.

"There is an auto parts store down the road. I can take you there and buy you a new one."

"Okay."

"Wait, why don't I take you miss?" the man who had stopped first asked.

"I'd rather go with Nathan because I know him." The man grabbed Avery's arm.

"Let go of her," Nathan growled. The man backed off. He glared at Nathan, then Avery. Feeling defeated, he walked to his car and pulled back out onto the freeway.

After Avery had locked up her car, she and Nathan went to the auto parts store. After finding an oil cap they went back to Avery's car and Nathan twisted it on for her. Avery didn't seem to notice Nathan's glances at her. She stood there beside him quietly.

"Do you want to grab something to eat before you go?" Nathan asked.

"Sure why not?" Avery was ravenous and dehydrated.

"Follow me out. I know the perfect place." Nathan replied.

Avery followed Nathan through Garland, Texas. She was happy to be in a cool air-conditioned car again. He took her to downtown where he had an apartment. The apartment complex was run down: the beige brick was worn out, the balcony railings were rusted, and the hedges needed to be trimmed. Avery was a little disgusted by the place.

"Hey I thought we were going to eat?" Avery asked. She stepped out of her Honda looking confused.

"Yeah, I am going to cook you something." Nathan replied. Avery decided to follow him. She was curious about him. Nathan was a popular jock back in high school and he was still attractive now a year later.

"I hope it's good!"

"It will be." Nathan opened the door of his apartment and Avery went inside. The apartment was cleaner on the inside than the outside. The carpet was beige and a huge curtain covered the sliding door. The walls were a light yellow color. Nathan walked over to the sliding door and pulled the curtain back.

"It isn't the best place but I like it."

Avery decided to play it safe and sit on the dark brown leather couch in the living room. She glanced around the apartment. It was comfortable and quaint.

"I think you have a nice place," Avery commented.

"Thanks. So what have you been doing since high school?" Nathan asked. They began chatting and catching up. As he was cooking, Nathan took off his polo. Avery looked away shyly at first, but he flashed her a toothy smile. Even his teeth were perfect. Nathan was a gym rat and his body reflected it.

"Like what you see?" Nathan asked. Avery shyly looked at the ground. The couple started to eat the burgers Nathan made.

"Wow!" Avery was impressed. This was one of the better burgers she had ever tasted.

"You like it?"

"Yes, it's so good." Avery took a bigger bite of the burger.

"I'm glad." Avery and Nathan munched on the meal until they were both satisfied. Avery went back to the couch.

"I am actually tired after eating that excellent burger. I should probably go home."

"No, stay for a while. You can sleep on the couch."

"Hmmmm okay."

Avery dozed off sleepily. Nathan had plans of his own. He let Avery sleep for a little while before initiating his plan.

"Oh…" Avery said, waking up. She looked down between her legs. Nate had his face between her legs. Her shorts were nowhere to be seen.

"How are you doing sleepyhead?"

"Okay. Where are my shorts?"

"Come on now. The way you dress you are just asking for it," Nathan replied. He started to kiss her thighs. Avery still felt a little drowsy. She pushed Nathan's head away. He pushed back continuing to kiss her thighs.

"I really don't want to do it with you, Nathan." He started kissing her stomach and her breasts.

"Are you sure? You picked me over that old guy." Avery was still feeling drowsy and helpless.

"I really think I should go home now." Avery started to get up.

"No, stay with me. I will make you feel so good," Nathan said cradling her with his muscular arms.

"Fine." Avery stayed. She was nineteen now. She would have to lose it sooner or later. Nathan seemed like a nice enough guy.

"Do you have a condom?" she whispered.

"Yeah, I do." Nathan started to kiss her. Avery let him. His mouth tasted like minty toothpaste. Nathan pressed his body onto hers. Avery kissed him back harder. She could feel his growing erection. Nathan let out a groan. She felt something wet on her skin.

"Owwww," he said. Avery opened her eyes.

Nathan was staring at her with his green eyes. He was in

shock. His trim stomach had been cut open by a small hand that extended out of Avery's stomach. It held his intestines tightly. His mouth oozed with blood. Avery could see the life going out of his green eyes. She grabbed the small hand but it was too late. It whipped around and grabbed her throat. Avery wrenched away. The hand was covered in blood. She choked under the pressure of the small hand. Avery struggled with it, finally falling off the couch onto the floor.

"I have been waiting a long time for this," a voice said.

She woke up out of the dream in a sweaty mess. Avery sat alone in her room at her mother's house. That dream had been going great until that hand came out of her stomach and attacked Nathan. It was something out of a horror movie. The alarm was blaring on her phone. Avery leaned over to shut it off. She laid back in bed for a second more. She didn't want to go to work. All she wanted to think about was Nathan but every time she thought about him the hand would show up in her mind instead of his face. There was a loud banging on the door.

"Hey!" Avery's brother yelled through the door.

"What?" Avery answered.

"Stop using the toilet in my bathroom. Every time you flush it, you happen to fuck it up. Use mom's bathroom or the downstairs bathroom."

"Okay!" Avery yelled back. She sat in her bed thinking of class. She still had a few more things to do for her Japanese host speech. She got up and stretched. Even with the nightmare, the sleep had felt good. She walked over to her white wooden computer table. She glanced at the old Dell she had been using. Avery got a little jealous thinking of all the college students with their nice new Mac laptops. And here she was with a big chunky ancient Dell laptop. She opened the lid and pulled up her presentation. She was very excited about her speech topic, host clubs in Japan, which she had learned about from a documentary. The speech was a masterpiece, or so she thought. She made a couple of changes to the pictures and words on the PowerPoint slides.

After taking a shower and getting dressed, Avery headed off to her college campus in the old Honda Accord she shared with her family. The only one of them who had any money was her sister Anna, a former stripper who had married a wealthy older man. Avery was oblivious to her own appearance. She was very pretty, petite, and well proportioned, as some would say. Her long black hair was healthy and shiny. Her brown eyes were the color of a hazelnut. Today Avery wore ripped jean shorts and a white tee shirt to school. She was also wearing high heel black Crocs that her sister had given to her.

In class everyone was chattering and waiting on the professor. Avery sat next to her friend Hannah Hayes. Avery had known her since freshman year of high school. Hannah had it all. She had long and fiery red hair and huge cobalt blue eyes that gleamed all the time. She was thinner and not as well proportioned as Avery, but she had an asset that attracted many boys' attention: her chest didn't fit her body. Her dad was also extremely wealthy and paid for everything. Avery, on the other hand, was on financial aid since there was no way that her family could help her pay for college. Her father had been dead for five years. Her mother was a nail shop manicurist. Avery worked at her mother's nail shop from time to time to make the family some more money as they struggled to pay the bills.

"Hey, so did you get my text?" Hannah asked. She twirled her long wavy red hair around her fingers. Some of the boys on the other side of the classroom kept glancing at her. Hannah was oblivious to this fact. Avery couldn't help but stare as well. Hannah had worn a tight tank top that enhanced her chest. On top of that she wore tight jeans as well.

"No, my phone is messed up, I think," Avery replied. She opened up her black Motorola Razor. Sometimes people at the college snickered at her for having such an old phone.

"You need to get a new phone, Avery."

"I can't. This is all I got okay." She was irritated at Hannah. She always had the best gadgets. Her father kept her spoiled because she was an only child. Avery was a little jealous of Hannah's iPhone and Mac laptop, but she knew that Hannah hadn't earned any of it. Avery had had to work about six months at the nail shop to get her Razor. She cringed thinking of all the dirty pedicures she had to deal with. Some women's feet were never meant to be seen.

"Good morning everyone!" Professor Simons said aloud. She went up to the chalkboard and wrote down today's date: March 5th, 2014. She also wrote the agenda for the day, which was persuasive speeches. She was a rather large woman. She wore tight black pants today and a floral theme shirt. Her brown hair was cut short like a man's. Avery was fond of Professor Simons because she was a foster parent to five children.

"Alright who is first for today? Get up to the podium and set up," the professor barked.

A timid boy stepped up and hurried to the podium at the front of the classroom. He seemed frazzled. The boy wore blue jeans and a top from the store Buckle. It was black with strange silver designs on it. He turned the PC on and made sure the PowerPoint was appearing on the projector screen at the front of the classroom.

The persuasive speeches dragged on until it was finally Avery's turn. She stood up in front of the classroom feeling bare and naked. She was extremely nervous. This was not how she had practiced her speech in front of the mirror. Now she had a real audience. Hannah gave a huge smile of encouragement. It was easy for her to not be the one front and center. The professor in the corner of the room was already jotting down notes.

"So I decided to make my persuasive speech about host clubs in Japan," Avery was finally able to muster up. She went on to describe how the hosts were the Japanese versions of male strippers, although they didn't take their clothes off. After her speech Avery walked proudly to her desk. She thought she had nailed it.

"Good speech, I want a hunky Japanese guy now," Hannah whispered in her direction. Avery giggled and hit her on the thigh.

"You wish. You know you would never date an Asian guy. Remember you are only into black guys."

"Just to piss off my dad. I have to say those black guys are pretty hung," Hannah replied giggling.

"No talking!" the professor barked, as the next student began his persuasive speech.

After all of the persuasive speeches were done for that day, the professor finally let the students go. She had asked only for Avery to stay behind. Avery walked over to the professor's desk with her head hung low. She knew she must have done something wrong when presenting the speech.

"Alright Miss Tran, how are you?" Professor Simons asked. The class had finally left the classroom. Avery was feeling hot and nervous.

"I am okay."

"You should loosen up. You didn't do anything wrong."

"I didn't?"

"No." Professor Simon gave Avery a piece of paper. "I decided to give you a sixty for effort." Avery was shocked. This was her first semester of college and she had never gotten an F up to that point.

"Why Professor? What was wrong with my speech?" she asked defensively.

"It was an informative speech, but not a persuasive speech."

"Okay…" Avery said, turning around. She walked out of the classroom and her face said it all. She was disappointed. She was also worried that financial aid would cut her off. Avery knew she needed an education to make it through life.

Avery walked to her car, which was hot from the Texas sun. She thought about how disappointed her mother would be. Avery turned on the engine of the car and started to go home. Sachse, Texas was not too far from Garland, Texas. In the car on the ride home, Venice appeared out of thin air. She wore a cleavage-baring red dress that was way too short for her and red platform high heels. Venice was Avery's imaginary friend, or so her family told her. To Avery she seemed very real. Every once in a while, Venice would come and comfort Avery when she was feeling down. Venice was Asian just like Avery. She was all hips and tits. Every time she appeared she would be wearing something glamourous. Back when Avery was younger, Venice looked to be her age and would dress the same as Avery. Now that Avery was older, Venice dressed differently.

"Don't worry about your financial aid. You're so smart, Avery," Venice said, sitting in the passenger seat. Venice wore her black silky hair up. Her tan body was glistening in the sunlight. Avery often thought if she would like to look like anybody it would be Venice. But Avery was much too modest to dress in Venice's provocative attire. Her brown soft eyes were covered with huge black sunglasses.

"I am not worried about it too much. I have a 3.5 GPA."

"You are a college girl now. You should go out and party and have fun with boys," Venice advised.

"No, I don't have time for boys. I've got to work at the nail salon. I've got assignments due."

"Suit yourself honey." Venice glanced over at Avery driving in the front seat. She gagged a little bit. "What is that outfit you're wearing? It's awful. Why don't you ever take my advice and wear something sexy?" Avery turned right on Fire Wheel Parkway. She was glad to be just a few minutes from home. She had another night class again today, after she was finished working at the nail salon.

"I don't want to wear something sexy because I don't have the body for it. I am lanky." Venice giggled.

"Oh, so oblivious to your killer little body."

"Look, I just need to focus on keeping my GPA up and saving up money."

"Your friend Hannah was dressed up really nice today," Venice said changing the subject. She never wanted to talk about working or classes with Avery. "I love the part where she said black guys are hung. You know what? You should fuck a black guy, Avery. Oh just think about how great it would be."

"No, I am not having sex with anyone right now."

"It would be so fun!" Venice started kicking her feet and posing provocatively, as if someone was taking glamorous photos of her.

"I just need to focus on me right now. Guys are the farthest thing from my mind." Avery turned into the driveway.

Her mother was waiting there for her. The family only had

two old cars that they shared with each other. There was silence in the car. Venice had disappeared as quickly as she had appeared, gone until next time. Avery's mother was dressed for work in tan stretchy pants and a black top with pink cherry blossoms on it. Her once black hair was now salt and pepper colored. She was as tall as Avery, although her stomach protruded out a little. It was leftover from the pregnancies. Her eyes were brown like Avery's and she had tattooed eyebrows. Somehow Avery's aunt had persuaded her mother into getting them.

"You're late. Mr. Troung will scold us," her mother said getting into the old Honda. Avery and her mother communicated in Vietnamese only.

"I know, mom. The professor told me to stay back in class. I'm sorry."

"Did you get an A?" her mother inquired. Avery continued to drive. Her mother scoffed loudly. All Avery could think about was how she didn't want to scrub women's feet. Especially if they were dirty.

At the nail shop Avery worked on cleaning and painting the toenails of large obese women. Her coworkers chattered around her in Vietnamese. The nail shop always had an interesting Asian aroma to it. In the corner was a large TV. It was always on the same channel. The channel consisted of people selling hair and beauty products. The obese woman currently in front of her was talking in Spanish loudly on the cell phone. She splashed some water on Avery's face accidently.

"I am so sorry," she said. She continued to talk on the phone in Spanish. Avery continued to scrape the dead skin off of her feet. It was never-ending. One time she had heard that in Thailand the massage therapist would bring out a fish bowl full of shiny minnows to feast on the dead skin on your feet.

Avery's mother was busy giving a French manicure to a customer on the other side of the salon. The salon was particularly busy with customers today. The Spanish woman kept splashing water at Avery. Her loud cell phone voice was extremely obnoxious. Avery could not wait until this pedicure was over. After Avery was done painting her toenails a neon purple color, the lady went off to let them dry. She stared down at them and started talking in Spanish.

"Where is your manager?" the lady squawked. Avery looked up from her black stool with surprise. The manager Mr. Troung had already come over and started talking to the obese woman. The woman complained about how this was not the color she had picked, even though clearly she had picked it and didn't like the way the color turned out on her toenails. Mr. Troung offered her a gift card and told her to come back. After the woman left, Mr. Troung turned his attention to Avery. She was already embarrassed that everyone's eyes were on her.

"Give me thirty dollars of your tips!" Mr. Troung demanded in Vietnamese. "Don't worry about what the other people think," he added. Avery reluctantly handed him the thirty dollars she had earned earlier that day. "Next time get the color that the client wants."

"Well she did want that color. I guess she didn't like the way the color turned out on her toenails."

"You giving me lip, girl?" Mr. Troung asked.

"No, sir."

"You're lucky I am only taking thirty dollars from you. I could take more."

"Yes, sir." Avery was grateful he spoke in Vietnamese so that the rest of the customers in the salon could not understand him. Her face was red from embarrassment.

Later on Avery's mother comforted her in the car and gave her thirty dollars of her own tips. She complained about Mr. Troung being an asshole but he was the only one keeping a roof over their heads. Avery didn't care. Once she got her degree as a registered nurse than she would never do nails ever again. She would be getting paid hourly, and have a regular salary. Then maybe she could support her aging mother as well.

Chapter Two

Venice's frigid breath

AVERY WAS HELPING HER MOTHER MUOI sort through pictures to create a photo album of the family. Avery couldn't take her eyes off one particular photo of her with her father in front of the old mobile home. The picture brought back old memories.

Five-year-old Avery nearly jumped out of her clothes from the noise. Her father staggered into the mobile home and knocked over the flower vase that he had just bought for her mom a few days ago. It was a "sorry I hit you" gift. Her dad's black hair was tousled and dirty. His eyes were bloodshot. His clean blue shirt was covered in what appeared to be vomit stains. Her dad's jeans were worse. They were wet from bottom to top.

"Come here you little shit!" He reached for Avery but she ran to her mother. Avery was scared when he was like this. Avery's mother didn't wait for her dad to respond. She threw tiny Avery over her shoulders. Her siblings ran after them into the master bathroom. Her mother placed Avery in the tub and her siblings climbed in with her. Her father banged loudly on the door.

"Fucking whore! Give me my kids!" Her dad kept yelling while trying to break down the bathroom door.

"Look." Her sister Anna pointed at a huge cockroach climbing on the side of the tub. Avery's brother Peter got some toilet paper and squeezed the life out of it. Her mother took the crushed cockroach and flushed it down the toilet. She then closed the lid. Avery's mother sat on the toilet and began to cry. Anna patted her back.

"It's okay, mom."

"When is it ever?" She continued to cry.

"Look I know you are in there, bitch! Give me my kids! Open the door!" Her dad yelled and banged on the door some more. He was panting heavily. It seemed like he was going to give up soon. Then Avery saw a girl in the corner of the bathroom. She was Asian and looked to be Avery's age. The girl approached her. She got in the tub with Avery and her brother Peter. Her brother did not seem to notice her presence. She soothed Avery by patting her back. Avery felt more relaxed. The girl smiled at Avery. She massaged her shoulders a little more. She opened her lips and spoke.

"You will be alright!" the girl said.

"How do you know?" Avery replied.

"I know."

"Who are you?"

"A friend."

"Mine or someone else's?"

"Yours, silly girl!"

Her mom stared at Avery. She looked angry and confused. Anna looked at her like she was crazy. Peter just stared at the tub.

"Who are you talking to?" her mother asked her after a long time.

"My friend."

"What friend?"

"She's right here." She grabbed the girl by the shoulders.

"You are grabbing air, stupid!" Anna laughed at Avery.

"She's right here!" Avery shook the girl one more time to show them.

"Are you that scared of dad? You would make up a friend?" Anna asked her, still laughing her head off. Avery's dad let out a loud snore from behind the door. Avery looked across at the girl again but she had vanished.

"I am not scared!"

"Yes you are!" Peter joined in with her. "Little Avery is scared of dad! She also thinks she has a make believe friend!" They repeated that over and over until her mother stepped in and told them to shut it. Avery couldn't help but wonder where her new friend had gone. After what seemed like a long while their mother let them out of the bathroom. Her dad was sprawled on the floor, sleeping peacefully. They were careful not to step on him.

Back in Avery's room, her siblings had fallen asleep and the Asian girl had come back. Avery was just about to fall asleep. The girl tapped on her shoulder.

"Hey," she whispered.

"Who are you?" Avery asked.

"I'm Venice."

"What are you?"

"I am your friend."

"Why is it my family can't see you?" Avery asked.

"They aren't special like you are," Venice replied. She started to stroke Avery's back. She couldn't shake this feeling off. Avery knew there was something not quite right with Venice.

"I am not special."

"Yes, you are. You have me."

"What?" Avery asked, confused.

"I really want to get out." Venice's voice started to get deeper and more demonic.

"Out of where?"

"You," Venice whispered in Avery's ear. Her breath was cold as her touch. Avery began to shiver. The room's atmosphere changed dramatically. It was darker and only a sliver of moonlight could be seen through the blinds.

"Please go away. You are scaring me." Avery held onto her blanket.

"I'll never be completely gone." The room was so frigid, Avery's teeth began chattering.

Avery's mother's voice interrupted her thoughts.

"Avery what do you think of this picture," her mother asked, bringing her back to the present day.

Avery glanced at the picture. It was a wedding photo of her parents. Avery shivered thinking of Venice. Ever since that first encounter, she knew Venice was a presence that couldn't be shaken off easily.

"Avery, are you paying attention?" Her mother asked.

"Yes, put it in the album. I have to go over to Hannah's house and do my sociology essay."

"Maybe I would get to know you more if you stopped hanging out with your friends," her mother replied angrily.

The drive over to Hannah's was relaxing. Hannah lived alone with her father since her mother had passed away when she was young. Avery pulled into the driveway. Hannah's house was bigger than Avery's mother's house. The property was located in the remote part of Sachse. The only neighbors were cattle.

"About time you got here," Hannah called to her from the garage. Her red hair was tied in a bun this time. She wore a tight cobalt blue halter top and black booty shorts. Avery noticed UPS boxes stacked to the side of the garage. This could only mean one thing. Hannah must have been ordering stuff in order to get the attention of Tai. He was her local UPS delivery guy. He was six foot two and just her type: tall, dark, and handsome. Hannah led her into the kitchen.

"Sorry, I had to take a shower," Avery replied. She had decided to wear loose fitting jeans and a red tee shirt.

"One day I am going to dress you up," Hannah replied looking at her outfit. "You have such a cute little butt. You should show it off more often." She slapped Avery's rear end after saying that.

"Hannah!" Avery yelped.

In the kitchen Hannah grabbed a blueberry yogurt from the fridge in the kitchen. She offered Avery some but she refused. She was lactose intolerant like most Asian people. Avery sat on a bar stool next to Hannah. The Hayes' kitchen was elegant. The stainless steel fridge gleamed as if it had been polished recently. The tile floor was sparkling as well. Hannah ate her yogurt quietly.

"Oh Avery I didn't know you were coming over today." Avery turned around to see Mr. Hayes. His hair was blonde and today it was messy. Mr. Hayes had a barely noticeable five o'clock shadow. He wore a light blue business shirt and dark blue boxers. Hannah almost leaped out her chair when she saw the boxers.

"Dad! What the hell! We have company! Warn us before you come out in boxers. Gross!"

"Well Hannah I need you to tie this tie for me. You are much more coordinated than I am."

"Alright, Alright! Just get in here." She ushered him back into the guest bedroom. Avery was left in the kitchen for a while. When they came back out she noticed Mr. Hayes was wearing black pants and a black tie. Hannah gave her the "Sorry my father came out in boxers" look.

After Hannah had fixed his tie, Mr. Hayes came back out of the master bedroom. His blond hair was combed back. He looked professional and very sexy as well. Avery's mouth was watering. She swallowed so she wouldn't drool.

"Don't mess up the house too much girls!" Mr. Hayes shut the garage door behind him.

Avery enjoyed the fact that Hannah's dad was so cool. He treated them well, almost as equals rather than children.

"Are you ready to work on our project?" Hannah interrupted Avery's thoughts.

"Sure."

"Alright then. Follow me."

Avery followed her through the living room, which had a beautiful black leather couch and a huge flat screen TV. There were a few pictures on the wall of the Hayes family before Hannah's mother passed away. Hannah led her down the main hallway and into her bedroom. The sheer size of Hannah's room never ceased to amaze her. The room was twice as big as her own bedroom. Hannah's ceiling was painted with an imitation of Vincent van Gogh's *Starry Night*. Hannah had painted it herself. Her ceiling was really one of a kind. When they were in high school she excelled in art. The rest of her room was filled with her own paintings.

"Alright so did you do any research on the founders of sociology?" Hannah asked sitting on her massive sleigh bed.

"I didn't really have to. All we are supposed to do is write an essay on their conflicting views." Hannah sighed.

"Well why don't you do that and I copy you." Avery sighed. Hannah was always looking for an easy way out. Hannah often gave blowjobs to the nerds in her classes to do her term papers for her.

"No, you are going to have to do the work this time. I am just here to help." Avery turned on her ancient dusty laptop. Hannah looked at it in disgust.

"Remind me to buy you a new laptop. It will be your Christmas present."

"Don't worry about that, Hannah. This laptop is still working."

"Whatever, anyway, so you have the book? I lost mine somewhere." Avery looked through her book bag.

"Yes, I have it." She pulled out her Sociology 1301 book.

"So guess what?" Hannah asked.

"What?"

"You know that creative writing class I am taking, right?"

"Yeah what about it?"

"The professor is so hot. I really want to fuck him." Avery sighed. Hannah was always ready to go.

"Can we get to writing now? This essay is due two days from now."

"Okay…" Hannah mumbled.

After writing three paragraphs about sociological theories, Avery laid back on Hannah's bed. Hannah was doing god knows what on her laptop. Avery once caught her watching porn when they were supposed to be writing an essay about the founders of sociology.

"Hey why don't we go to a bar?"

"Why?"

"You've got to reward yourself after working hard on your essay." Hannah started getting undressed in front of Avery. Hannah's body was model perfect. She could have modeled for playboy or hustler. She picked out a sequined short black dress. Avery watched with envy as the dress went over her beautiful red hair and curvy figure.

"I don't know. Let me see your essay."

"No, I am not finished." Hannah shut her laptop. She

didn't want Avery to see the sex tape she had made with a random guy from the college. She was watching it the whole time they were supposed to be working on the sociology essay. Hannah was a little bit of an exhibitionist.

"Okay, I think I am going home though."

"Why?"

"I don't want to go to a bar."

"Okay, suit yourself, but before you go. Does this make me look fat?" Avery could only laugh. Even girls like Hannah had low self-esteem.

"No, you are as beautiful as ever."

In the nail shop the next day Avery was working on an older women's nails, scraping off the dead skin. The manager Mr. Troung was yelling in Vietnamese at the other employees. The door opened and the familiar smell of overpowering perfume filled the shop. It was none other than Avery's sister, Anna Tran. Anna walked into the nail shop with a teacup snow-white Pomeranian in her purse. The critter barked a few times and panted with its cute little tongue hanging out. Mr. Troung looked at it with disgust. He didn't like cute furry things. The only reason he tolerated Anna is because she was his dream girl. Many of his nights were spent having wet dreams about his employee Muoi's daughter.

Anna wore a tight black leather corset and the tightest skinny jeans she could find. Her sleek long black hair was tied up in a ponytail. She was the complete opposite of the ordinary Avery.

"Hey mother!" Anna said in Vietnamese. She waved to her mother in the back of the store, ignoring Avery.

Avery continued to work on her customer's nails. Back in high school Avery lived in the shadow of her older sister. Anna had gone right into stripping after she graduated and then was rescued by a wealthy lonely seventy-year-old man. He married Anna but she didn't change her ways. One day Anna got drunk and told Avery everything about how she was cheating on her husband with the pool boy and all his executive friends. Avery never saw her sister in the same light.

"Hey little sister," Anna said, standing over Avery.

"Hey Anna? Do you want your nails done? Is that why you came in today?"

"No, I wanted to see mom and you, see what you guys were up to."

Avery squirted some lotion on the customer's hands and started to massage them. The old women laid back further into her chair and sighed.

"Nothing much, just working as you can see." The little Pomeranian licked Avery's ear. Avery giggled and tickled its furry chest.

"Keep your hands off my dog," her sister snapped. Truthfully, Anna was jealous of Avery. She was everything Anna wanted to be: a working college student, someone with a future.

"Fine." Avery went back to massaging her customer's hands.

Anna went to the backroom to talk to the other nail shop employees. The manager Mr. Troung was ogling her. His thick glasses made him look even more disturbing. Anna's chest was bulging out of her corset. Mr. Troung licked his lips thinking of all the nasty things he would do if Anna was his.

Finally Avery went back home. It was late at night and she was finishing her essay. After a long day at the nail shop and dealing with Hannah, she had to take a break and think about something else for a while. To her surprise this is when Venice showed up. She was wearing the same attire as Anna was earlier in the nail salon.

"Don't I look just like your sister Anna?" Venice said.

"Yeah sure, Venice. Can't you see I am trying to study?"

"Come on, don't be such a bookworm." Venice threw a book at her. It was *Crazy Rich Asians* by Kevin Kwan.

"I am not a bookworm, I just know if I do well in school then I will get my dream job."

"Fuck your dream job! Why can't you be like Anna? Be crazy and do drugs?"

"Because Anna is a delinquent. I am a responsible human being!" Venice sighed. Avery went back to typing on her ancient laptop. She felt leather on her chin. She looked up from the laptop to see Venice smiling gleefully.

"Now this is more like it." Venice held a long slender riding crop to Avery's chin.

"Really? You are so pushy, Venice." Avery tossed the riding crop to the side. Venice fell back on the black chair in Avery's room.

"You're so lame, Avery. Don't you want to be famous?"

"No, famous people are actually very depressed. I saw a documentary about it once." Avery went back to typing on her laptop. She would have to finish this essay with Venice in her ear.

"Anna's such a bitch. Why do you let her treat you like that?" Venice asked changing the subject.

"Well Anna is Anna. What I am supposed to do?" Venice sat up.

"Duh! You're supposed to act like you own the world and you're a badass." Avery was starting to get irritated. She had had enough of Venice.

"Why don't you just go away and leave me alone for a while?" She then proceeded to throw a pillow at Venice. She vanished with a puff. Now that Avery's blood pressure was really up, she started writing about Karl Max with a passion. She eventually grew tired. Avery was fading fast.

Avery woke up the next day with the sun shining in her face. She had forgotten to close the blinds. Avery had her sociology class to go to today. She could hear her brother Peter screaming in the other room. He had some of his friends over. They were playing some video game, but Avery needed to take a shower so she slipped past her brother's room.

"Is that your hot sister?" Avery heard one of his friends ask.

"Nope it's the ugly one," another replied.

Avery walked into the master bedroom to get ready for class. She was a little broken up about her brother's friends' comments, but she didn't let it get her down for long. Within a couple of minutes Avery was dressed and ready. She wore black shorts and a grey tank top. She grabbed her old beat up UT backpack. It was burnt orange in color and had a longhorn logo on it.

As Avery drove to Richland College, Venice appeared in the passenger seat. She had her black hair up like a geisha and wore a red provocative silky kimono that showed off her tan legs.

"So, how did you sleep?" she asked Avery, sipping what looked like a martini.

"I slept fine."

"Did you dream about anything?"

"Nothing interesting." Venice lifted her perfectly pluck eyebrow.

"Are you sure?"

"Nothing at all, Venice."

"So what are you going to do today?" Venice asked excitedly.

"I don't know. Go to class and work."

"You bore me, you know that?" Venice replied.

"What do you expect from me Venice?

"I expect only the best."

"Which is?"

"You go and model for Playboy." Venice looked off in the distance. As if she could envision herself being a Playboy model.

"How about you stop nagging me. You remind me of my mother."

"How dare you?" Venice asked looking hurt. She vanished again.

After Avery made it to the college, she realized how much her back was hurting. She had been having back pains for quite some time now. She stumbled out of the car. A group of girls nearby smirked. They couldn't help but laugh at Avery and her ancient car. Everything Avery owned was ancient.

A boy who had been dozing under a tree woke up with a grunt. He looked up to see a beautiful Asian girl walking towards him. Her long black hair whipped around in the wind a little bit. The black shorts and high heels she wore showed off her tan legs. Her almond eyes were full of life and curiosity. The boy decided to approach this mysterious Asian girl who he had never seen before.

"Hey good looking." This was the best line the guy could come up with.

"I'm late for class," Avery responded picking up her pace.

"What class are you going to?"

"Sociology 1301." The boy's brown eyes were full of curiosity. He wanted to know more about her.

"Hey stop for a second." The boy grabbed her arm. "Seriously stop for a second." Avery stopped and looked in the direction of the parking lot, which was where the boy was looking.

"So, you see that white bike at the end of the parking lot." Avery looked further down to see a white motorcycle. "If that was my bike would you ride on the back of it?" the boy asked. His tan hand grazed Avery's hip.

"Well first off my bottom is too big to fit on that small bike. It would look weird." Avery brushed him off and continued to walk to class. The boy stopped and watched her.

In class, Avery sat in her usual spot. Avery liked her professor. He was young, and smart, and was from somewhere in the Middle East so he had a little bit of an accent. That day they debated and talked about social groups.

After class Avery remained on campus. She was reading the book *Crazy Rich Asians* by Kevin Kwan. This book was scandalous and raunchy, but Avery loved reading every little drama-filled page. Her classmate Dana approached her. Avery had known Dana since high school, and considered her less a friend than an annoying bug that would not go away. Dana considered herself to be Avery's best friend but she was far from it. That day, Dana was wearing a short black skirt and you could almost see her bottom sticking out. Her blue tube top was even more revealing. She had acne on her face and chest. For some odd reason Dana thought she was the hottest thing that ever lived.

"Oh my god! Avery you wouldn't believe this but I had like two guys cum in me last night. I had to take a morning after pill to prevent pregnancy." People in the study hall began whispering. Avery laughed in her head. No wonder that Dana didn't have any friends.

"Good for you," Avery replied.

"Hey did I tell you I got a new job?" Dana smiled. She brushed back a lock of brown hair. "The job is so great. I buy pot from my manager and smoke it with her! Who can do that? Right?" Dana let out a loud obnoxious laugh.

"I could only imagine. Well look, Dana, I've got to go," Avery said getting up from the comfy couch she was sitting on.

"Oh, Avery, quit that nail shop job. Come work with me and smoke pot. All I do is sell lingerie to obese women. So easy, you will love it."

"I'd rather not be affiliated with someone who smokes pot."

"What the hell does that mean?" Avery stopped cold in her tracks.

"I mean, I don't want to see obese women in lingerie." Dana laughed.

"Oh me too, they are so gross, so many rolls."

"Anyway, I really got to go."

"Bye, bye!"

Avery got into her ancient Honda. She debated going back into the study hall or going home. She wondered if Dana would come back and bother her. She was embarrassed to be seen or spoken to by Dana. Venice appeared in the seat next to her. This time Venice was wearing a short sequined black cocktail dress and long gloves. Venice's long obsidian black hair was up in a tight bun.

"Can you believe that girl?" Venice asked.

"That is Dana for you."

"Gosh she is so stupid."

"I know. She'll get knocked up and miserable sooner or later. I am glad that isn't me."

"Hey, what about that guy from earlier?" Venice said placing her hands on her hips and huffing.

"What about him?"

"He was a very cute black guy."

"Kind of nerdy if you ask me."

"So you could have asked him on a date. He was totally putting the make on you."

"Come on, Venice. Get real!"

"What does that mean?"

"I am an average Asian girl at best."

"No, you're not, you are fucking beautiful! If only you dressed up and combed your hair!"

"I don't have the time to dress up. You know it takes Hannah two hours to get ready to go somewhere. I am not going to be one of those girls." Venice punched Avery in the arm.

"Then what type of girl are you going to be?"

"I am going to be Mulan, Asian warrior princess."

"So what type of girl are you going to be?" Venice asked louder.

"Mulan, Asian warrior princess!" Avery clutched her hand in a fist and punched the air. Venice smiled knowing she had empowered shy Avery for a moment.

An older Caucasian couple in a Corolla looked over at Avery and they stared at each other. The couple had been watching Avery since she left campus. They found it odd she was talking to herself. The woman opened her mouth first.

"What is that Asian girl doing?"

"I have no idea," the husband replied.

The couple sped off as the light turned green. They didn't want to be near that strange Asian woman who talked to herself and punched the air. Avery and Venice antagonized each other all the way home.

Chapter Three

The Ordinary Avery

AVERY STEPPED OUT OF THE OLD HONDA. The campus was busy as usual. Boys and girls sat on benches talking amongst themselves. A skateboarder passed Avery. She noticed that the number of college boys skateboarding around campus was rising. Today she had work right after classes and she wasn't looking forward to dealing with Mr. Troung. The other day he had taken away more money from her without any good reason. Mr. Troung just liked to bully his employees since he knew most of them wouldn't report him for taking away their money. Avery debated reporting him but she knew it wouldn't do any good since he would just take away more of her tips.

Avery walked into her sociology class where she found Anna waiting and sitting in her seat. She was chatting with one of Avery's classmates. Anna smiled at Avery. She thought Avery's outfit was tacky: an orange top with a decorative flower on it and black capris. Avery knew that Anna was out of place on this college campus. For one she wore a tight tan mini skirt and crème colored top with go-go boots. The two sisters could only stare at each other.

"What are you doing here?" Avery asked sliding in next to her sister.

"What do you think I am doing? I am a student here," Anna responded proudly. The truth was Anna had gotten in through making a massive donation to the school. How else could she have gotten into Richland College in the middle of the semester?

"So what do you know about sociology?"

"Nothing, that's why I'm here to learn."

"Oh yeah?"

"Yeah." Avery felt something hit her on the back of the head. A boy in the class threw a piece of notebook paper at her wadded up in a ball. She picked it up.

"What is that for?" Avery yelled at the boy.

"Leave the hot new chick alone, you skank." The boy was Latino and already in love with Anna.

"Whatever," Avery responded and opened her textbook. Anna had been there for less than two seconds and now the whole classroom was against her. She could hear them snickering and refused to look up from her textbook until her professor came into the class.

Today's class subject was about deviance and social control. The professor lectured and debated with the class about crime and statistics. He talked about how if there were no criminals how many people would be without jobs. He talked about how a society with no social control would fall apart. How laws were needed in order to control society. Avery listened and participated but she also watched Anna out of the corner of her eye. Anna was texting the entire time. Avery laughed knowing that there would be a quiz at the end of class.

"Alright, take out a piece of paper. You have a quiz today." The class moaned. There was a flurry of movement as everyone gathered the materials. Anna jumped off her phone. She freaked out at the word quiz.

Anna looked over at Avery's paper. She couldn't read upside down. Avery smiled at her.

"Having a little trouble there?"

"No, I am beautiful and smart. I don't need your help," Anna hissed.

"Beautiful maybe, smart no. You just wanted to copy me. You knew you wouldn't make it past your first semester."

"Ya? Well at least I have a husband who is going to take care of me for the rest of my life."

"You don't even love him. You've cheated on him how many times?"

"Hush! No talking during the quiz."

Avery turned back to the board where the questions were posted. This would be an easy quiz since Avery took good notes and listened carefully absorbing the professor's every word. Anna struggled with the questions. She didn't know which answer to pick for the question Anna was confused. By the time the class ended she had just scribbled down gibberish. Avery had gotten every one of the questions correct.

"Alright class you are dismissed. See you next week," the professor said after collecting all the quizzes. The sisters raced out of the room, and Avery tripped over an object on the floor. She fell to her knees.

"Bye Avery." Anna said. She kicked Avery's ratty old purse away from her. Anna walked away with a smug look on her face.

"Wow, that girl is vicious," commented a voice behind Avery. She turned back to see a girl with damaged brown hair and blue eyes. She had many brown little freckles on her face. Avery wondered why she hadn't noticed this girl before.

"No kidding, that chick is my sister."

"Oh, no way! You guys don't even look the same. "

"Tell me about it. She is a stripper you know. I am never going to be affiliated with anyone who is a sex worker."

"I'm Reagan," the girl said introducing herself.

"I'm Avery." She smiled and shook the girl's hand.

Avery and Reagan talked on and on. It turned out that Reagan was a nursing major too. She was going to help her aunt that weekend at a nursing home and she invited Avery to join. After thinking a minute, Avery said she would. Reagan was different. She came from a large Jewish family. She loved food, reading, and taking care of people. She also had a bitch of an older sister, although her sister sounded much worse than Anna. Avery and Reagan plotted on how they would succeed and be better than their older siblings. They talked about how fun it would be to be nurses working in the same hospital.

Avery sat in the nail shop. It was really hot today and the air conditioner was broken so Mr. Troung left the door open. A few customers came into the nail salon in spite of the heat. Avery was taking a break and sitting in front of the automatic fan. The cool breeze it produced helped Avery cool off. Mr. Troung was swearing up and down in Vietnamese. He was yelling at the air conditioner repairman. The poor repairman was sweating and hunched over the unit. He was avoiding Mr. Troung's spit. Avery's manager loved to spit when he talked.

"So Avery. How was school today?" Avery's mother squeezed in next to her. She talked in Vietnamese so that the customers couldn't understand what they were saying.

"Pretty good mom, did you know that Anna is going to college?" Avery's mother laughed.

"Anna?"

"Yes, my sister Anna."

"No, is she really?"

"She's in my sociology class." Avery's mother chuckled.

"Interesting, I am sure she will do great!" Avery coughed. Anna had lied to their mother about her scandalous past.

"Yeah, sure mom. Can I ask you something? Are you happy with the children you have?"

"Sure. I wish I had more." Avery's mother looked sad after answering her question.

"What's wrong?"

"Nothing, dear."

"Oh come on something is going on."

"Well your question brought back some memories from the past. Memories that I had suppressed for a while."

"What memories?" Avery's mother looked off into the distance.

"Before you I had a miscarriage," she said softly.

"What? Really? You did?" Avery was shocked that her mother would tell her something so private.

"Yes. Well, it wasn't exactly a miscarriage. It was a stillborn baby. It took me a while to work up the courage to have you."

"Why, what happened?" Avery's mother still stared into the distance. She looked very solemn and depressed. She took a deep breath before she answered.

"Your father and I buried your sibling under the old mobile home."

"What? Why?"

"We didn't have enough money at the time for a proper funeral."

"Oh, so nothing happened." Avery's mother looked more upset.

"Well after we buried your sibling, I started seeing things. I started seeing things that weren't there." Avery started to shiver. She knew all too well where this was going.

"Seeing *what* that wasn't there?"

"I saw a baby rocking back and forth under a chair. It had no eyes." Avery's mother took a deep breath mustering up her strength. "It watched me and terrified me from afar. This happened for about a year." Avery's mother finished speaking but by then she couldn't control it. Tears streamed down her face. "My baby, my baby, my baby," she cried. Avery comforted her mother. She rubbed her back and tried to calm her down.

Mr. Troung had noticed her mother crying. His face was red and sweaty from the heat. His circular spectacles gleamed in the bright light of the salon. He wore a plaid pullover with a white short sleeve shirt. His pants were mustard colored. He walked over to them in the hideous ensemble.

"What are you crying about, Muoi?" Mr. Troung asked. Avery's mother kept crying and couldn't answer. Mr. Troung turned to Avery.

"Get her out of here please. We don't need her crying in here. Take the day off, but don't forget to give me twenty percent of the tips you made." Avery groaned. She quickly gave him what he wanted and rushed her mother to the car.

"Feed her some Pho. She might feel better," Mr. Troung added. Pho is a popular Vietnamese noodle dish. Avery decided to follow Troung's advice and took her mother to a popular Pho restaurant in Dallas. After eating, Avery's mother felt better. She didn't mention the stillborn again. Avery knew better now. She still thought about why her parents would bury a stillborn under the mobile home. She wondered if the ghost of the baby still haunted her mother from time to time. She shuddered thinking of a baby with no eyes rocking back and forth. Avery went home after eating dinner. Her mother retired to her own room and Avery lay down in her own bed. Her thoughts were interrupted by a text on her phone from Hannah. She wanted to meet. Avery was worn out but agreed to join her at a local Starbucks.

The Starbucks was a popular joint for the high school kids in the area. Avery had ordered a green tea Frappuccino. Hannah walked into the Starbucks. On her arm was a tall attractive black guy. His chin was sharp and his arms were toned. He wore a black t-shirt with vulgar language on it. His head was bald. Avery didn't know if he had shaved it by choice. He had pushed his faded blue jeans down intentionally so you could see his faded blue boxers. Hannah with this mysterious boy and ordered a drink. She smiled and waved to Avery. Her male escort did the same.

As soon as the couple got their drinks, they sat down in front of Avery. All she could do was smile. She was not at all shocked to see Hannah with a black guy since she had met some of her boyfriend before. But everyone else in the tiny coffee shop couldn't help but stare. The small-town patrons didn't approve of Hannah's date. Hannah, however, loved the attention. She loved setting the crowd apart. Then she could pick out who was against and who was with her. Her grandfather had told her once before that "I want people to have an opinion about me. If they don't have an opinion about me I go up and kick them in the knee. At least now, I know they have an opinion about me." Hannah smiled, thinking of her aging grandfather's comment.

"I'm Jerome. It's a pleasure to meet you." Hannah's date shook Avery's hand. His voice was deep. Hannah spoke up after forgetting to introduce her date.

"This is my boyfriend," Hannah said, grabbing on to Jerome like he was precious stone.

"He certainly seems…" Avery stared at Jerome's tattoos, which consisted of odd symbols and designs. "Nice."

"Thanks," Jerome said shyly.

"So Jerome is a bouncer at a local club. I forgot the name but that is where I met him," Hannah said.

"It's called Jaguars," Jerome corrected Hannah. He pushed her long curly red hair back. He felt really lucky to be with this girl. The other girl he had been with before her was what people call a "big, beautiful woman." Hannah was the perfect size, however, curvy and with the most beautiful blue eyes.

"Isn't that a strip club?" Avery inquired.

"Yeah, they pay me pretty good there," Jerome replied.

"So are you doing anything else besides being a bouncer at a strip club?"

"I am a repo man on the side."

"Oh." Avery looked down at the table and took a sip of Frappuccino.

"Yeah, I like bouncing better. The repo deal. You got to sneak around and stuff." Hannah gazed up at Jerome.

"Isn't he just wonderful?" she asked.

"Perfect," Avery replied. She really thought Jerome was very average.

"So, Hannah told me you're going to be a nurse. Are you ready to see blood?" Avery gulped.

"I can stand the sight of blood. I think I will be fine." Jerome took a sip of passion fruit tea.

"My aunt is a nurse. She makes a lot of money. I was thinking of going to college again and majoring in engineering." Avery looked up shocked by what she had just heard.

"You went to college before? Where did you go?" Jerome coughed.

"I had a full ride to SMU." Southern Methodist University is an elite college in Texas. Avery was surprised that Jerome had gotten in.

"Oh my god! Why didn't you stay?" Jerome stared at his cup. Hannah answered for him.

"His grandmother got sick and is dying of cancer. He needed to get a job immediately. He is the one paying the bills for her treatment."

"I am so sorry to bring up such a sore subject," Avery responded.

"Don't worry about it. You didn't know any better. I sure do miss that full ride though. Working at the club and repoing business is not ideal. I would rather work on building bridges, cars, and buildings."

They continued to talk on into the evening. Avery was already feeling tired from the day. Jerome revealed more about himself and his troubled childhood. He came from the projects of Detroit. His mother was a drug addict and his father had died when he was young. His grandmother had raised him since he was seven. Avery felt sorry for him. She still had at least one parent. All this boy had was his dying grandmother. Eventually the group parted ways and Avery went home.

At home Avery ate dinner, some stir fry and rice. She watched TV for a while. After it turned dark, Avery felt drowsy and wandered off to bed where she fell into a deep sleep.

The next day Avery sat in traffic listening to the radio. She was downtown and late for her meeting with Reagan. The car in front of Avery happened to be a monster truck. It wasn't uncommon to see them in Texas. It roared to life and rolled a few inches forward. Avery rolled up her window. Another nice day ruined by the black smoke coming from a truck.

Avery arrived at the nursing home where Reagan and her aunt worked in downtown Dallas. Reagan's aunt ordered Avery to put on a pair of scrubs, which she did in the bathroom. She came out ready for her first task. Reagan's aunt was nice but very bossy. The nursing home was full. In the rec center, seniors sat around watching TV. There was an exercise room where the older ladies did some light yoga. Avery's first task was giving the residents their pills. Reagan's aunt had already put the pills in a cup and made sure they had the right amount of medication. She watched Avery like a hawk. Technically what she was doing was not legal but she knew her niece and her little Asian friend wanted to be nurses. This would give them some experience.

An older gentleman who had been diagnosed with dementia refused to take his medication. He tried to attack Avery. The man was a Vietnam veteran and called Avery some nasty names. The orderlies were forced to restrain him and apologized to Avery.

"Sorry about that Avery, that guy is always like that with everyone." Regan pushed her damaged brown hair back. She had covered up her brown freckles with make up today.

"Don't worry about it. So this is what we are going to be dealing with when we are nurses."

"Yep, the good, the bad, and the downright ugly."

"I agree."

Avery's next task was to clean out the bedpans. It was the absolute worst job she could think of. Avery choked and gagged as she hosed down the bedpans. She hoped when she was a real nurse she wouldn't have to deal with cleaning bedpans. They were trying so hard not to get the waste on themselves. Reagan's aunt laughed seeing Avery and her niece struggle to clean out the bedpans. She had to do this task daily.

Avery's next assignment was to watch as Regan's aunt took some blood from the residents. The elderly woman shuddered as Reagan's aunt approached with a long needle. Avery felt sorry for the poor woman. She didn't like needles either. She knew she would have to test patients' blood as a nurse. Reagan's face went white as soon as her aunt mentioned blood. Avery knew she didn't want to deal with blood either.

"Please not this time. I am not in the mood," the elderly woman said.

"Come on, Mrs. Bennett," Reagan's aunt said.

"No, I don't want to."

"You have to. We have to test your cholesterol level and other things. Make sure you are okay."

"I really don't want to," Mrs. Bennett growled. Reagan's aunt crept closer. Mrs. Bennett squirmed in her wheel chair.

"Don't you get any closer, I will bite." Reagan's aunt tried to stick the needle in her arm. Mrs. Bennett ended up biting her. That ended the day at their retirement home.

Avery and Regan decided to have lunch after the ordeal. They went to a popular Mexican restaurant in the area. They were seated right away.

"That was an ordeal," Reagan said after ordering.

"Yeah, I can't believe your aunt got bit."

"She is used to it. Imagine if she was a dentist."

"I am sure she would get bit even more."

"Yeah, so what do you think now? Still want to be a nurse?" Avery thought for a second about the prospect of cleaning bedpans, distributing pills, and dealing with unruly patients. It all sounded so awful.

"I couldn't think of a better job. It is so fulfilling!" Avery lied.

"Yeah, whenever I am free I try to go to the retirement home and help out. I think by far the worst job is cleaning out those bedpans."

"Yuck, can we talk about something else?" Reagan thought for a minute.

"How is your sister?"

"We haven't talked much."

"Oh, so how's working with your mom?"

"Pretty good, I like the nail shop but I hate the boss."

"What makes him so terrible?" Avery began to rant about Mr. Troung.

"For one, he looks like a creep. Two, he takes a large percentage of my tips. Not just mine, but all of his employees. He is always complaining about how I paint nails and stuff. It gets annoying quick. You should have seen what he wore the other day. He has a terrible fashion sense." Reagan laughed.

"I am sure it was not that bad."

"Oh yes it was. Plaid and mustard colored pants."

"That does sound awful."

The plates finally came and the new friends ate. They chatted and got their complaints out in the open. Avery finally hugged Reagan goodbye. She had made a great friend. She was glad she met Reagan when she did. Driving home, Venice appeared in a rubber band-tight white mini dress. Her long black hair was curly. She looked like she was ready for a night out on the town.

"Reagan seems nice," Venice said.

"She is nice."

"So how are you feeling today?" Avery thought for a minute. She wanted to ask Venice if maybe she was the stillborn from earlier.

"I don't know. I feel terrible about my mother..." Avery started.

"Yes, your poor mother. Having to go through that terrible ordeal. Why would she bury the baby under the mobile home?"

"I wanted to ask her." The car began to get colder. The temperature plummeted a few degrees. Avery shivered. She turned the air conditioner down.

"You know it is almost like your mother didn't care about her children." Venice replied.

"No, don't say that!" Avery argued.

"Why not?"

"She does care about her children."

"She does too." Avery replied. Venice's skin began to turn black. She was full of rage and resentment.

"Then why does she try to get rid of them unsuccessfully?" Venice retorted.

"What do you mean?" Avery asked.

"Nothing... I have to go..." Venice disappeared quickly as she came. Avery was disturbed by the turn of events. What was Venice trying to imply?

Chapter Four

Venice Revealed

Avery and Hannah were shopping at one of the local malls. Hannah had just broken up with Jerome. She was feeling very depressed. Avery decided to be a great best friend and take her shopping. They were passing through the Barnes and Noble. Avery was waiting on Hannah to get out of the bathroom.

Out of the corner of her eye, she saw something. Avery turned around to see a large poster of woman in her forties wearing a beautiful black suit. Her hair was blond and her eyes were light blue.

Come Meet Pennie Apples! Renowned Police Psychic!

She is here for a one day book signing for her new book
Silver Spoon

Pennie's book signing is at 4:00 pm on Friday
in the sci fi section.

Please come with an open mind!

Hannah came back out of the bathroom. She strutted over to Avery. She glanced at the poster.

"Wow, she looks great! Psychic too. Pretty cool," Hannah said giving Avery her take on the poster.

"Who really knows? I'm going to buy her book," Avery responded. Hannah tapped her foot impatiently waiting on Avery. After Avery grabbed her green bag from the cashier, she and Hannah set off to Sephora.

Their eyes widened at the sight of the cosmetics that lined the shelves of Sephora. Hannah went straight for eye shadow and Avery had her eyes on the lipstick. Hannah started trying on the eye color cosmetics. She felt like a kid in a candy store. Her self-esteem was beginning to rise again. Soon she would forget all about Jerome. Avery decided not to try on the lipstick since she was very self-consciously clean. One time a girl asked to use her lip gloss in the bathroom. Avery immediately threw away the tube after the girl had used it. She even had to wash her hands afterwards. She studied a plum colored tube.

"Would you like to try that on, Miss?" the sales girl asked. She was wearing all black. She looked so fake down to her eye-lashes.

"No, I am just looking."

"Okay, let me know if you need help with anything else."

Hannah came over. She was sporting the smoky eye look. Hannah was a beautiful girl, so she didn't need make up but when she wore it, she was the spitting image of a runway model.

"Let's go to Bath and Body Works. Be quick, they close soon."

"Okay, but let's buy at least one thing."

Hannah and Avery headed over to Bath and Body Works. They sprayed each other with perfumes and washed their hands in the polished sinks. They loved going into the store just to spray the perfumes and act like imbeciles. The clerk was entertained by them.

Hannah dropped Avery off at home. Avery felt a little drunk from all the perfumes she was wearing. The scent was very strong. She lazily climbed the stairs. Every step Avery grew sleepier and sleepier. Her brother's friends were playing their video games again. They were loud and obnoxious, totally oblivious to people being in the house. Avery crawled into bed. It was nice and cold. She drifted off into a deep and disturbing sleep.

Avery woke up. The sun was shining in her face. She stretched and got up. She had a long day ahead of her. Today, Avery was going to work and school. She jumped into the shower, and cleaned herself up.

Avery stepped out of the shower minute later. She wore black pants and black tank top with a silver flower design on it.

She stepped out of the bathroom feeling refreshed and ready for the day. She was met by a smack to the side of her face. Avery sat there for a second dazed. Her brother stood in front of her. He was about five foot two with a mustache and messy black hair. Your typical Asian gamer, he had chip crumbs all over his face and pimples on his forehead. The only features the siblings had in common were their brown eyes.

"You didn't pump gas in the car. The car was empty and I had to call my friend to pick me up." He kicked Avery in the stomach. She was still dazed from the blow to her face earlier.

"What? I did fill up the car?"

"Whatever. You're such a pain in my rear." Her brother Peter walked away with a smug grin.

Avery lay on the ground holding her face and stomach. She contemplated running after him and taking her revenge. Hitting him wasn't going to do anything though. Avery thought about what would hurt him the most. Maybe she would throw his PlayStation out the window.

Avery hurried to the car. She didn't know a bruise was forming on her cheek. She sped off to class but as soon as she stepped foot on campus, people started to stare. Avery shook it off. She didn't notice the bruise. She walked into the hall smiling, thinking about how she would destroy her brother's PlayStation later. Avery sat by Reagan on a bench with the students waiting for the professor. Her brown hair was frizzy and dry. She wore khakis, a green polo, and black-rimmed glasses today.

"What happened to your cheek?" Avery looked at her wondering what to say.

"I tripped and fell. Nothing to write home about."

"Really? It looks fresh and it's getting darker by the minute."

"Well do you have any make up?" Regan shuffled through her purse.

"I have some foundation."

"That will work, let's go to the bathroom real quick."

The other students murmured and pointed at Avery's cheek. In the bathroom, Reagan helped Avery cover up the enormous bruise on her cheek. Avery's face dropped as soon as she looked in the mirror. It didn't feel like her brother had hit her hard at all. Looking back she remembered that it stung a little. Reagan was a good friend. She quickly pulled out the foundation and applied it.

"Who did this to you?" Reagan whispered. Avery wouldn't look into Reagan's green eyes. She didn't know what to tell her.

"I fell and tripped down the stairs at my house. It's nothing really."

"Okay, but you don't have to put up with this, you know." Avery smiled.

"Oh, I am going to break his PlayStation."

"Are you sure you don't have anything to tell me?"

"I'm sure. Just ignore it. Let's go to class."

Avery walked back to class thinking of what she would tell her mother. She decided to tell her the truth and see what she would say. Today, the class talked about gender and sex. They talked about how women made less income than men. They talked about gays and lesbians. The professor showed a few clips from youtube about the subject. Avery noticed her idiot sister Anna was sitting by the Latino student who was smitten with her. She was still annoyed with Anna. She knew she only liked the status and prestige of being a college student. But when it came to writing APA and MLA essays, she had no clue what to do. Avery smiled secretly knowing her sister would suffer, especially in the statistics class she would be required to take.

After class Avery drove to the nail salon. Her mother was already working on a customer's French manicure. The customer held a phone in her other hand chatting away. She was overweight and had a double chin. Mr. Troung was staring at the women intently. He was wondering when she would break the chair. Avery's mother Muoi nodded at her as she walked by.

"What have you been doing all day?" Muoi asked her.

"You know, working and going to school."

"Well, you are doing well. Your dad would be proud."

"Speaking of dad, do you remember the memorial held for him?"

"What about it?"

"I was thinking about it. Where is his body?"

"We had him cremated after the accident."

"The urn is empty."

"I threw his ashes on the grounds of his favorite bar."

"Okay, it makes me wonder."

"Wonder what? You want your father to be alive?" Muoi asked.

"No, that would be awful."

After Avery and her mother arrived home Avery broke down and told her everything about her bruised cheek. Her mother was infuriated. She disliked the fact Peter was becoming more like his father every day. Muoi went upstairs and threw open Peter's door to his bedroom. He looked up from the monitor to see his mother was glaring at him. Out of instinct he clung to his precious PlayStation.

"No, mama, don't! I love you!" he screamed as Avery's mother threw the game console out the window. She flung it across the yard, and out into the street where a car ran it over.

"No!!!!!!" Peter yelled running outside to retrieve the battered PlayStation.

Avery went to bed satisfied. Justice had been served. She could hear her mother and brother arguing downstairs. Avery crawled into bed. She wasn't sleepy just yet. She decided to pick up the book she bought recently, *The Silver Spoon*. She read the back cover, her curiosity piqued. She immediately grabbed her laptop and started looking up Pennie Apples. The first thing that showed up was her book and also a few newspaper articles. The first one was about a six-year-old girl who went missing from her family home in New Orleans, Louisiana. Pennie Apples had helped the Federal Bureau of Investigation find her body in a matter of three days. According to this article, Pennie drew elaborate sketches that pointed in the general direction of the girl's body. Pennie's very first case had been in Austin, Texas. There, she had helped the Austin police department find the missing mother of a two-year-old, Tara Vanderbilt. It turned out that her husband had been frequenting with drug dealers in the area. He ended up doing something to the wrong one. Pennie's fifth case was just as interesting. It started in Mexico. A high-ranking drug kingpin hired her to find his daughter Lisa Gomez. The daughter was found later beside the highway somewhere in Mexico. Her most recent case had started in Los Angeles, California, where a family man by the name of Smith Thompson had gone missing, and led to Moscow, Russia, where he had showed up dead. According to the article he had slept with someone's wife in the Russian mob. They killed him and the cheating wife. Pennie found the hit man as well as the bodies. The physic detective obviously knew what she was doing. It was interesting that she worked through sketches and touching the victims' personal belongings. Avery closed her laptop. It was getting hot from being overworked. She laid back and immersed herself in the soft covers. She dreamed again that night.

She was six years old. Her father had left fresh bruises all over her body. Avery was in her room crying. Her siblings had been lucky not to be sick that day. Avery wiped the tears off her face with her blanket. She knew better. She knew she should have kept out of his way. Avery was hungry and wanted something to eat. This was why she woke him up. Her dad was upset and still drunk from the whiskey.

"Are you okay?" she heard a voice say behind her. Avery looked over to see Venice. The Asian girl walked over to Avery and started to stroke her back. Her touch was cold as usual. This girl wouldn't leave Avery alone.

"No..." Avery said, suppressing tears.

"It's okay. Everything is going to be okay," Venice whispered.

"How do you know? You aren't even real." Avery could feel the excruciating pain in her back. The fever came back. She had managed to make this girl angry once again.

"I am real!" Venice screamed at the top of her lungs. Avery could feel Venice's cold hands grasp her around the throat.

"Please… Let go…" Avery managed to say. Venice continued to stifle her windpipe.

"Say I am real! Say you will be my friend."

"Alright… I will be your friend." Avery felt Venice's grasp weaken.

Avery looked up to see Venice staring at her. She looked malevolent. She flashed Avery an evil smile.

"Why do you want me to be your friend so bad Venice? Why?" Avery asked.

"You are all I have. I don't have anyone else to talk to," Venice replied. She didn't seem as malevolent now.

"I am really all you have?" Avery asked.

"Yes, I have no one else to talk to…" For the first time Venice looked vulnerable and harmless.

"So, friends?" Venice asked extending her hand to Avery. She shook Venice's cold hand and made her a promise to be friends forever.

Avery woke up from the dream. It was a memory she had suppressed some time ago. She had forgotten all about their deal. Avery was beginning to wonder why Venice had stuck around all these years. If she was truly an imaginary friend, wouldn't she have left years ago? Avery was beginning to think Venice was something else. Something more than just a figment of her imagination.

"Hey there!" a voice interrupted her thoughts. Avery glanced up to see Venice. She was dressed in a provocative tight dark blue dress. It had lacy sleeves. The dress made every angle on her body pop. This time she materialized with heavy blue eye shadow. On her feet were suede blue booties.

"Wow…" Venice smiled.

"I know, don't you love this dress and my hair." Venice' hair was curly and tied up in loose ponytail which she pulled forward.

"You look great!"

"Yes, I know."

"I have a question Venice." Avery pushed her covers off and turned on the fan.

"Go ahead and ask me." Venice replied. She snapped her fingers and a long white cigarette appeared. She took a deep breath and inhaled the cigarette.

"Why are you still here?" Venice did her best not to look startled.

"I am here because I am part of you."

"What do you mean?" Avery asked. The room was starting to feel chilly. Avery started to feel the old Venice emerging again.

"I am your sister." Avery coughed.

"What do you mean my sister?" Venice's face began to distort.

"I mean your sister. We are twins." Avery began getting a splitting headache.

"Twins? Twins? What do you mean twins?" Her headache did not subside. In fact it grew worse. The room was a blur.. "Tell me Venice, tell me what you really are?"

"I just told you. Accept it. You are part of me and I am part of you." Avery started to feel dizzy.

Chapter Five

The Ancient Mobile Home

AVERY WOKE UP. She carefully examined the room around her. Everything seemed intact. Nothing out of place. What did Venice mean by saying that she was part of Avery? She was confused. Why was Venice so angry? Then Avery remembered the stillborn. Could Venice be the ghost of the still born? Avery's head was spinning. She was anxious to find out what Venice was. She needed to be sure. She called Hannah to help her.

"Hey, you awake?" Hannah asked. She was on the other line.

"Yes, what's up?"

"Can I come over? There's something I need to tell you."

"You can't just tell me on the phone?"

"No, it is important."

"Seriously, it is so early in the morning."

"Alright, see you soon!" Avery hung up.

The sun started to rise outside. Avery managed to get up and make some tea before Hannah arrived. Hannah texted Avery to let her in. The two went to the kitchen where Avery handed her a cup of peppermint tea. They sat down face to face at the tan wooden breakfast table. Hannah was wearing a red hoodie and dark blue skinny jeans. She looked really good considering it was so early in the morning.

"So what do you want to tell me?" Hannah asked. She took a sip of tea.

"Would you mind driving with me to Tyler today?" Hannah looked amused.

"You woke me up for that?"

"There is something I want to show you," Avery said. She was thinking of the still born underneath her childhood home.

"What?"

"Something very important to me."

"It's early in the morning. Just tell me."

"Look, I want to show you my childhood home. There is something there. I want to show you. Will you come with me or not?"

"Fine," Hannah replied, giving in.

After putting on a blue hoodie and white tee shirt, Avery put on sneakers to go with her skinny jeans. The two headed out for Tyler. Avery and Hannah drove in her red Porsche. Avery liked this because this way she didn't have to pay for gas. Plus, Hannah drove. The two talked about their childhoods.

Hannah had spent a year in Argentina when she was about six years old. She had spoken fluent Spanish back then. Avery told her about her chilling past. She told her about the beatings her father would give her daily. She told her about the decaying mobile home. Avery revealed that her father died of alcohol poisoning. Hannah had never known about this before. She was shocked to hear these stories since she had always envied Avery. After Avery told Hannah everything there was to say about her past, she stopped and thought for a little bit. Hannah was silently driving to Tyler. She was thinking about what the old mobile home would look like.

"That will be forty dollars and fifty-eight cents," the guy behind the register told Avery.

Avery and Hannah had made a pit stop to get gas. She remembered this old gas station. Her mom and dad used to refuel here after long trips. The gas station was now run down. The dirty floor needed to be mopped. There was a neon sign pointing the way to the bathroom. The guy behind the register was even more revolting than the gas station itself. He had zits and pimples all over his white face. Avery kind of felt sorry for him. He flashed her a yellow toothy smile before she walked out the door. Outside Hannah was staring at the woods on the other side of the gas station.

"Are you alright?" Avery felt uneasy. They were surrounded by thick oak trees. Today was a cloudy day in Tyler, Texas. The clouds looked like rain would pour out of them at any minute. The wind stirred the oak trees. It howled and rustled the branches.

"I feel fine, lets go." Hannah drove down Highway 110. The road had been modernized so there were more commuters. The landscape was now filled with new country homes and mobile homes. Avery thought briefly about her dad driving down the highway at night before it was new and industrialized.

Before, Highway 110 was a typical back road. The trees created a tunnel to drive through. It was beautiful in the daytime but at night it would play tricks on your eyes. After driving for some time. Avery spotted the old place she used to call home.

"Pull over there." Avery pointed to her family's old mobile home.

You could barely see the old mobile home through the thick and green overgrowth. The chain fence surrounding the property was covered in honeysuckles bushes. The scent coming from the honeysuckles was familiar but not comforting. The only part not overtaken by plants was the opening of the fence that Hannah and Avery drove through. Hannah pulled her red Porsche onto the property and Avery noticed that the grass was also quite thick. Avery told Hannah to park in the old outdoor garage. It was not attached to the mobile home and was the only object not overtaken by weeds and shrubbery. Hannah parked the car and glanced in Avery's direction.

"I can't believe you lived in that shabby mobile home!"

"My family was poor back then."

"This is inhumane! You shouldn't have lived under these conditions at all."

"I know, but like I said we were poor."

"I would never live here!"

"Anyways, let's explore the trailer."

"Sure, what are you hoping to find?"

"Something my mom and dad buried here years ago." Avery reached into her bag for the red plastic toy shovel that she had found in the garage earlier that day.

"We are using *that*?" Hannah looked amused. Avery didn't answer her. She didn't see what was wrong with the red toy shovel.

"Wait, bug spray. I brought it just in case," Avery said before they walked any further. She sprayed Hannah down with it. Hannah reciprocated.

Grasshoppers hopped out of the way as they walked through the tall grass toward the mobile home. The mobile had once been white but now it was a pale yellow color from years of abandonment. The old porch had been torn down by the weather or vandals and was now just a stack of wood. A set of concrete blocks had been stacked on top of each other in a makeshift staircase leading up to the front door of the mobile home. Avery wondered if someone was living in it. Looking up close, she saw that the windows were all broken in and covered with trash bags. The old oak tree out front was charred and dead. It had obviously been hit by lightning. As Avery remembered there were small holes on the side of the mobile home where the walls had buckled from the weight of its occupants.

Hannah and Avery walked up to the trailer. A gust of wind came blowing through and shook the old mobile home. Hannah nearly took off but Avery stayed put. She needed to get her hands on the still born her mother buried all those years ago.

"So, we are going to have to crawl around down here," Avery stated staring into the black abyss under the mobile home. She took a flashlight out of pocket and shined it under the mobile home.

"What? Why? I am too scared. Go by yourself." All of a sudden they could see a truck turning into the lot of the old mobile home. Avery quickly pushed Hannah under the mobile home. The dark chill sent shivers up Avery's spine and it smelled like death and decay. The dirt under the mobile home was soft and wet and there were cobwebs everywhere. Accompanying the cobwebs were mushrooms. There was something that flew by Avery's ear. She flinched and swatted it away.

They heard the truck pull into the driveway of the mobile home. Hannah and Avery watched from underneath the mobile home. Two men stepped out of the car. It was zit and pimple face from the gas station and he had brought a friend. Pimple face was wearing his blue shirt and jeans. His friend was wearing a loose-fitting white shirt, jeans, and a cowboy hat. His buddy had a bat in his hand.

"I think they are in there. That is the red car I saw earlier!" the guy from the gas station said.

"They better be or else!" His friend looked mean. He had a farmer's tan and was sporting a huge scar across his forehead.

"I promise, Fred. I want the Asian. You can have her cute little redhead friend though."

"I don't like Asians anyways. They nuthin' but a plague."

They started walking toward the mobile home. Hannah and Avery backed up. Avery knew she had to get to the miscarriage before they were discovered.

"They aren't in there. You are good as dead my friend." Pimple face's friend had a gravelly voice.

"They are in here buddy. Trust me that is their car right there!"

"Better be! I want me some pussy tonight!" Hannah squeezed Avery's hand. She could feel her heart pounding in her ears.

"There will be tons of pussy tonight!" Pimple face had brought his friend to rape them.

"Better be." Avery heard the door of the mobile home open and close.

Beneath the mobile home Avery scrambled around. She kept the beam on the flashlight low. She remembered her mother mentioning something about burying the miscarriage near the refrigerator on the mobile home. Avery started digging frantically in the soft dirt. Hannah was whimpering behind her. She couldn't believe the situation she was in. Up above in the mobile home the men were stomping around. Avery continued to dig frantically with the flashlight in her mouth. The tip of her plastic toy shovel hit something and Avery saw it. The shoebox. It was the shoebox that held the body of her dead sibling. Avery quickly dug it up.

"Alright, I got it, now listen to me," Avery whispered to

Hannah. "Give me the car keys." Hannah gave her the Porsche keys. "On my count we will run to the car. I will drive. You just need to get in the passenger seat. Okay?" Hannah nodded. She couldn't bring herself to whisper back. Avery crawled to one of the entrances beneath the mobile home.

"One, two," she whispered. Suddenly something landed on her face. She felt a quick smack and whatever was on her face was gone. Her face was wet. Avery shined her flashlight over to see a big toad staring at her. Hannah yelped.

"Did you hear that?" the two girls heard above them. It was pimple face's friend.

"No, what?"

"Sounded like a yelp?"

"What, really?"

"Keep searching this piece of shit. We'll find them."

Avery held Hannah's mouth to further prevent her from making noise. She put the toy shovel and flashlight down. She had her hands full with the box and keys.

"Three, now I want you to run as fast as you can to the car," Avery whispered.

The pair took off from underneath the mobile home. Avery almost lost her grip on the shoebox. The grasshoppers were flying out of the way to avoid them. Hannah got to the car first. It was already unlocked. Avery rushed in after her. She threw the shoebox in the passenger side of the car. Hannah screamed as Avery took off down the driveway. Pimple face and his friend heard the commotion outside. The two were making a mad dash for their beat up white Chevy truck. Avery didn't waste a second. She drove as fast as she could down the road to the highway. Avery looked behind them. There was no white pickup truck following them. She sighed in relief. Hannah was still screaming and staring at the contents of the box. Avery pulled over. She hugged Hannah for a while until she finally calmed down.

"I can't believe you just dug up a body. What the fuck, Avery?" Hannah said after she calmed down.

"It's not really a body." Avery picked up the fetus in the pink blanket it had been wrapped in. She placed it back in the shoebox.

"Not a body? Well what the hell is it?"

"It's my sibling."

"What the heck is going on?" Hannah asked.

"My mom had a still born before me. She buried it under the mobile home. Now, I dug it back up." Avery shrugged. It seemed pretty simple to her.

"Why did you dig it back up?"

"I just want to give my sibling a proper burial."

"Avery you are crazy. You could have gotten us murdered back there. All for a body."

Avery and Hannah drove back in silence. They decided to bury the stillborn baby in a local park. Avery recited a prayer and built a cross made out of sticks to mark the grave. The disheveled Hannah dropped her off at home. She took off back to her own home, disturbed by the day's events.

It was still grey and dreary outside when Avery entered her home. After the events of the day all she could think of was taking a nap. The house was quiet. Her mother was probably still working, and she had no idea where her brother was. She laid down in the soft sheets thinking of how close they had come to being killed. Those men back in Tyler meant business. She and Hannah had to run at full speed to get away. Avery started feeling guilty for dragging Hannah along. She wondered if Hannah would ever forgive her. The poor girl had been shaking like a leaf.

After arriving home, Avery took a long well deserved bath. She thought maybe Venice would be gone after burying the still born. She would have to make this up to Hannah. Avery crawled into bed and drifted off to sleep.

For the next few days, Avery went to school and work like normal. Venice had not bothered her since the day she had reburied the stillborn. She felt she was truly free from Venice now. Avery woke up startled by a knock on her door.

"Who is it?" Avery asked through the door.

"Your mom, get up we are going to be late for work."

"Okay, mom," Avery replied.

She stepped out of bed. Avery was still dirty from yesterday. She walked into her closet and picked out some clothes. Today she decided to wear dark navy pants and a crisp white long sleeve shirt. After showering and getting cleaned up, she made her way downstairs where her mother was waiting. Her mother was wearing a loose fitting yellow shirt with pink flowers on it. She wore loose blue jeans to go with it. Her black hair was curled slightly. She looked good for an older woman.

"So you're finally ready?" Muoi asked.

"Yes, let's go."

In the car Avery was silent. She kept thinking about the still born and Venice. Venice had not shown up since she had buried the newborn. She buried the poor thing and recited a prayer. She thought she had done everything right. Was there something she missed?

At the nail salon it was a busy day. A bridal party had come in to get their nails done. Mr. Troung micromanaged everyone keeping the drunken bride and bridesmaids in check. Avery was servicing a very delirious bridesmaid. Her blond bun was loose and strands of blond locks hung all over her neck. Her blue eyes were dilated and her face drooped a little. She had very large breasts. Avery knew they had to be implants. This girl didn't have any fat on her. Avery was giving her a pedicure so she started by filing off the dead skin on the bottom of her feet.

Avery listened to this girl talk about cheating with her best friend's fiancé and partying all night with the bride. Avery asked her how she made a living. The girl laughed and replied that she was a porn star. She did about ten films a year. She went on to tell Avery about all the men she had been with and how fun it was. Avery was nothing but disgusted with this.

After the large bridal party had left, Mr. Troung handed his employees a percentage of what the bridal party had given him.

"How is Anna doing?" Mr. Troung asked.

"I haven't seen her in a while."

"I heard she is going to school."

"Sure, but she isn't going to last long." Mr. Troung coughed.

"Anna is beautiful and smart! How dare you say that about your own sister?"

"Oh, she's just a perfect little angel you want to wrap in your arms? Isn't she?" Avery said sarcastically.

"Perfectly proportioned. Not too big and not too skinny."

Avery walked back to the table in the nail salon. She sat down to wait for more clients. Mr. Troung was drooling now, daydreaming of Anna again. A fantasy that would never happen. The day dragged on as more customers came and left. Avery was getting weary. She worked on her essay for sociology whenever she had free time. Finally the day was over. Avery swore that if she looked at one more nail she would go berserk.

"Come on dear, let's go home," her mother said.

"Alright, I am pretty tired. You want to just grab chicken on the way home?"

"Sounds like a great idea!"

Avery and her mother went home. They chatted about the almost intolerable drunken bridal party and the women with the disgusting feet. Her mother was sure a woman had farted during her pedicure. Avery complained about Mr. Troung. Both women wished they had a boss who wasn't creepy. After chatting with her mother, Avery wandered off to bed.

She switched on the light to see Venice sitting on her bed. She was not upbeat and positive as she usually was. She didn't wear anything provocative. She was rather demure, wearing a simple black dress.

"So look who it is," Venice said, smiling at Avery. Her smile sent shivers down Avery's back. She was the last person Avery expected to see.

"I thought... I thought you were gone..." Avery stammered. The lights started flickering on and off.

"Oh you did? You thought I'd never come back after burying that thing?"

"That thing was you, wasn't it?" Avery asked.

"I am here. Guess your little plan didn't work after all."

"What are you? Why won't you leave me alone?" Venice snorted.

"I am your twin! I have told you already."

"I don't understand," Avery said. She had backed up into a corner of the room. Venice stood over her menacingly.

"Why did you try to get rid of me Avery? Am I that bad?" Venice asked.

"No, no, no," Avery repeated.

"Then why? I thought we were friends?" Venice said with a deep voice. Her hair whipped around.

"Just leave me alone, get out of here! Get out of my life!" Avery screamed at the top of her lungs. She closed her eyes, and prayed Venice would leave forever.

"You'll regret this Avery…" Venice whispered in her ear.

After sometime, Avery glanced up to see no one. She was relieved. Maybe Venice was gone for good now.

Chapter Six

Ninth Heaven

Avery drifted off to sleep.

In her dream, Avery was seated in a large auditorium. It was dark and the only light came from the stage. She recognized Venice immediately. Venice wore a traditional Vietnamese dress. It was a long sleeve dress with an elaborate gold flower design. The set was made up to look like the Vietnamese countryside. She dramatically fell to her knees. She started talking.

"It has been so many years since I have seen my one true love. The Vietnam War tore us apart. I see him in my dreams. His young face always made me feel safe. It has been twenty years since the war ended. I always wondered what happened to him. I lost him in the chaos in Saigon all those years ago."

"Linh, I am here." A man called out. He walked into the spotlight. He wore the old army uniform from back during the Vietnam War. He took off the green helmet. Venice stopped crying. She ran into his arms.

"Oh Duc it has been so long! Where have you been?"

The elderly women next to Avery whispered in her ear. "That is the world famous Asian actress Venice Tran. She's absolutely beautiful isn't she?"

"Actress?" Avery responded.

Avery woke up to the smell of cigarettes, marijuana, and sweat. Loud clubbing music played in the background. She was a little groggy but sat up. She rubbed her eyes. People were all over the place. The men and women were completely naked and left little to the imagination. In the bed closest to her,

Avery saw a brunette woman injecting a brown substance into a man's vein. In the bed to her left, she was shocked to see a man with a large python around his neck. The snake was about four feet long, and hefty. Its brown eyes stared into Avery. She was worried it might eat her but the snake was not interested in her. The man's brown eyes were bulging. The snake seemed tame and was only squeezing the man enough to give him a thrill. A woman with blond hair sat on top of the man, naked and bouncing away on top of him. Her face was intense. She was slapping his face, saying, "You like, that don't you? You liked being chocked, don't you bitch?" The woman kept bouncing on the man and he seemed to be enjoying it. The snake squeezed his neck a little harder. He grabbed his partner's breasts squeezing the life out of them. His partner yelped, but she enjoyed it. The man let out a roar after the python tightened its grip.

Avery started to get up. Then she realized something: she was completely naked. She quickly grabbed the red sheet on the bed and covered herself. She heard moaning in the corner. A nearby couple was sexually exploring each other. Avery looked away embarrassed. There was a huge fireplace on the other side of the room. A group of men and women was stationed in front of the fireplace on a giant bearskin rug, fulfilling their amorous appetites. A huge chandelier was positioned above illuminating the room. In the other corner of the room was a door that was left open. The music was coming from there. Avery made her way over to the door. She stepped over couples making love, completely terrified and uncertain how she had gotten there. All she could remember was falling asleep in her own bed.

"You're awake, amour!" A man stepped out in front of her. His face was concealed by a latex hood and his genitals were covered with leather underwear. Avery quivered at the sight of him. She tried to pass him but he wouldn't let her through.

"Who are you?"

"I'm Daniel. Don't you remember me? We made such sweet love tonight," Daniel replied, grabbing her by the hips.

He spoke with a strong European accent.

"I am sorry, I don't… Do you know where my clothes are?"

"Over in the closet, amour."

"Thanks." Avery wriggled out of his grasp.

"Not so fast, amour. Don't you know I want to make love with you again?"

"I'd rather not." Avery was trying her best to get out of his strong grip.

A woman came out of one of the oak wood doors near the fireplace. The woman had her blond hair tied up in a ponytail and was wearing dominatrix clothing. A pair of thigh-high tight leather boots encased her legs and the rest of her body was covered in a black latex suit. Her face was very stern but she was out of this world beautiful. Her deep green eyes pierced into your soul. She stared at Avery, then Daniel.

"Daniel, you escaped before I could punish you," the woman said. She slapped her black whip into her palm.

"I am sorry, Cecelia. I am coming, like a good slave." The man in the latex hood walked back over to his master. She smacked his back sharply with the whip leaving a mark.

"As for you, don't come near my slave again," the woman warned Avery as she walked back into the dungeon. She shut the door behind her.

Avery shrugged at this and walked into the closet. She shook her head. What did that guy mean by making love with her? Avery would never have sex with a man like that, not even if someone paid her. What was this place? Why were the people naked? Why were they dressed in latex and leather? Avery found her car keys in the pocket of her black winter jacket. It wasn't cold outside but Avery put on the winter jacket and some tights she had found that looked like hers. She couldn't be sure. The closet was a mess. There were latex and leather outfits everywhere. Avery made her way through a door and stumbled upon a dance floor. There was DJ playing music in the corner and people were dancing naked or wearing under-garments. There was a makeshift bar in the corner and a large disco ball rotated above. A large neon sign illuminated the room with the words "Ninth Heaven."

She left the club feeling vulnerable and weak. Avery was startled when she looked back to see a large mansion. She was standing in one of Dallas's ritziest neighborhoods, Highland Park. You would have never known driving by this house that it was a swinger's club. A large bouncer stood at the door of the mansion. He had long blond hair and wore a black suit. His height was staggering.

"Hey, you wouldn't happen to know where I parked, would you?" she asked the bouncer.

"Everyone parks at the school across the street," he replied with a thick accent.

Avery made her way across the street to the school. It was an elementary school. She finally found her ancient Honda. She got in and took a breath. She couldn't believe that she had woken up in a swinger's club. She would have to tell Hannah. Avery thought about the last thought she had had before going to sleep. She was thinking about the term paper for one of her classes. She never in a million years would have thought she'd end up in a swinger's club a few hours later. She shook her head and started the car.

After driving for a little bit, Avery was able to find her way home. When she opened the garage, her mother ran through the door. She was disheveled and had woken up from the sound of the door creaking open.

"What are you doing out here so late, Avery?" She glanced at Avery's coat. "What are you doing wearing that coat? It isn't winter."

"It's a long story mom."

"Well, where were you?"

"I don't want to talk about it." Avery started walking up the stairs.

"You smell."

"I know."

"Were you doing drugs with your friends?" her mother asked, sniffing her jacket.

"No, mother. You know me, I'm a good kid."

Avery made her way upstairs. Her mother followed her.

She had stopped questioning her and walked into the bathroom. Avery got up to wash her face but when she walked into the bathroom her face dropped. In the reflection of the mirror was Venice. There was no doubt about it, she was the spitting image of Venice. Avery's hair black hair was wavy. She had on very dark eye shadow and bright red lipstick. Black mascara was thick on her eyelashes. Avery quickly walked over to the sink and washed the makeup off her face. Walking back to room, Avery couldn't return back to sleep. She knew Venice must be real. She wasn't just some figment of Avery's imagination. Venice somehow controlled her while she slept. Dawn broke and she quickly called Hannah.

"Hello?" Hannah said from the other line. She sounded angry that Avery had woken her up from her beauty sleep.

"Hannah, it's me!"

"Avery, what do you want so early in the morning?"

"Hannah, I don't know where to start. It's Venice. She is, she is… Controlling me." Avery said quickly.

"What are you talking about Avery?"

"Venice, she is real! She isn't imaginary. She's real. She's alive!" Avery said urgently.

"What are you talking about?" Hannah asked impatiently.

"Venice, she was my imaginary friend… Sibling… I don't know…" Avery responded.

"Look, I am coming over. I have no idea what is going on. You sound crazy."

"Please come over as soon as possible. I don't feel so well."

Avery sat in her bed thinking about what to do. She was worried about her wellbeing. Perhaps she was losing her mind. Avery had never told Hannah about Venice before, but now it was different. Avery didn't want her best friend to think she was a freak because she had an imaginary friend. After seeing herself in the mirror, Avery knew she had to act and fast. She thought about the stillborn baby. Avery shook her head. Nothing made sense to her anymore. One minute, she was chasing ghosts. Then she ended up the exact replica of Venice. Avery got out of bed after a couple of minutes. A sharp knock on the door indicated Hannah was at Avery's home.

Avery opened the door to find a very irritated Hannah wearing dark grey cotton shorts and a silver t-shirt with the word "dream" on it.

"Come in," Avery said, pulling her in quickly.

"Sheesh! So early in the morning." Hannah yawned. Avery sat on the beige couch in the living room. Hannah sat next to her.

"I just don't know what is going on."

"What do you mean? What happened to you last night?"

"I.. I woke up in a swinger's club." Hannah laughed.

"You? Oh come on…"

"Seriously Hannah!"

"Okay what was the club called?"

"It's called Ninth Heaven. I think."

"Oh," Hannah responded. "Well how did you end up there?"

"That's what I have been trying to tell you." Avery sighed. This thing with Venice was spiraling out of control. What would she do next? Should she sleep at all anymore? "Venice is controlling me," Avery finished.

"Who is this Venice and why haven't you told me about her before?"

"She's my friend. No one else can see her but me." Hannah remembered the incident at the old mobile home.

"Omg, you're telling me this Venice person is the reason you dug up that dead body in Tyler?" Avery started to cry.

"It wasn't a dead person. It was my sibling!" Hannah started to comfort her and pat her back.

"Alright well what do you suggest we do then?"

"I don't know…" Avery said. Hannah thought carefully for a second. If what Avery was telling her was true, then they could only do one thing: an exorcism to rid Avery of this malevolent entity.

"Look, where is your laptop?" Hannah asked after Avery stopped crying.

"It's right here." Avery handed her the laptop. Hannah grabbed it in disgust. She looked at the keyboard which had missing letters and numbers.

"How am I supposed to work with this thing?" Hannah asked.

"What do you need to look up?" Avery asked, curious to hear what Hannah was thinking.

"Look up 'exorcisms in Dallas, Texas.'" Hannah said sharply. Avery did as she was told and typed it in.

"Ah, here we are. Click on the craigslist ad," Hannah commanded after skimming through numerous websites.

The craigslist ad was as blunt as could be. It had a picture of a cross and holy water. The person who wrote it offered to do exorcisms on people who were possessed. The person also guaranteed the demon would be exorcised forever. All this for only one hundred dollars.

"What hundred dollars? I don't have that kind of money," Avery responded after seeing the ad.

"You don't, but I do," Hannah said after hitting reply.

"What are you doing? Are you really going to respond to this person?"

"You say you are being controlled." Avery sighed. She didn't really have much of a choice. She needed to get rid of Venice.

"Alright, you should be rid of whatever this Venice is," Hannah said after replying to the ad.

"I hope this works."

The person who put the ad up called herself Madame La Belle. Avery and Hannah headed over to the location she gave them. The neighborhood was filthy. It was in one of the lowest income neighborhoods in Dallas. They took Avery's car to be safe. Hannah didn't want her precious Porsche being broken into. The houses had chain linked fences and broken windows. Stray dogs ran around the neighborhood in packs.

"I'm scared," Hannah admitted after Avery parked the Honda.

"Me too…"

"You still want to go through with this?" Avery nodded in response to Hannah's question.

She stepped out of her Honda and headed to the sanctuary

of the house. The house in front of them was small. It had bars over the windows and door. Avery rang the doorbell. The door slowly creaked open.

"Who is it?" A woman asked. Avery and Hannah jumped back. The barrel of a shotgun pointed in their direction.

"We are the girls from the ad," Avery said quickly.

An elderly woman stuck her head out. Her face was wrinkled and her most distinct feature was her glass eyeball. It was a dark blue color. Her other eye was black. She wore a ratty old brown shawl with an outdated dress that belonged in the 1800s.

"Ahhh!" Hannah said looking at the misshapen glass eye ball. The woman pushed the girls inside the house.

"Sorry about that girls. You never can be too sure around these neck of the woods."

"It's alright," Avery responded. She glanced around the house. There was pungent odor coming from the kitchen. The odor was foreign to Avery. The house was dark. The old women had left all the blinds down. The only light came from a dimly lit candle.

"Come along," the woman said.

They walked into a dark room. There were some dolls in the corner. A large bookshelf took up the other wall. Avery shivered. What had she gotten herself into? The elderly woman sat down on a winged Victorian chair. She lit a pipe.

"So which one of you is the possessed?" she asked.

"I am," Avery piped up.

"You have the money?" she demanded.

"Here," Hannah said handing her the hundred dollars.

"Alright let's get it started." She took the dimly lit candle and started to light smaller candles on the floor with it. As the light began to brighten the room, Avery saw a red pentagram painted on the wood floor.

"What the heck, are you a witch?" Hannah asked.

"No, why would you think such a thing?" Avery and Hannah looked at each other.

"Why do you have a pentagram painted on the floor?" Avery asked.

"That is part of the exorcism."

"Okay…" Avery said quietly.

"Don't worry about a thing. I am the Madame La Belle after all. A qualified exorcist."

"Now please lay down on your back on the floor in the middle of the pentagram please."

Avery did this. She wondered what qualified Madame La Belle. She wondered if this exorcism would truly remove Venice. The wood floor was cold, Avery turned over to see the pile of dolls. Most of the dolls' hair had been replaced with candy such as Twix and Snickers.

"Why do you replace the dolls' hair with candy?" Avery asked.

"I sell those dolls to people," the woman responded. Avery turned back and stared at the ceiling. She couldn't imagine what type of people would buy those demented-looking dolls.

Madame La Belle pulled open a container. It smelled horrible. She began to paint on Avery. She squirmed away after the cold liquid hit her face.

"What are you doing?" Avery asked.

"I am putting chicken's blood on you. This is part of the exorcism." Avery calmed back down. She let the woman cover her with the chicken's blood. Hannah looked on, happy not to be participating. Then La Belle started painting symbols on the floor. Avery sighed. The chicken's blood smelled awful.

The elderly woman took a dusty book from the bookshelf. She began to recite something in a foreign language. She sprinkled more liquid on Avery. The room remained dimly lit. The candles flickered. The house was quiet except for the elderly woman chanting. Hannah whimpered. She was afraid. She didn't know what was going to happen. The suspense was killing her.

"Why is nothing happening?" Avery asked, interrupting the woman.

"I don't know. Maybe you are not possessed, as you think you are. Let me get some ox blood."

The woman walked out of the room leaving Avery and Hannah alone. Avery thought about wiping the chicken blood off her face. After a little while the woman came back. Hannah shrieked, which caused Avery to sit up.

"Oh quiet, it is just a mask," she said, pulling off the wooden mask from her face.

"Why do you need that?" Avery asked, laying back down. The mask was horrifying. Avery understood why Hannah was frightened. It was wooden and had two round holes for the eyes. Feathers were glued to the side of the mask. They were different colors ranging from a canary yellow to a dark red. The mask was painted with symbols and letters.

"It was a gift from a witch doctor in Haiti. It is an artifact that is supposed to help in exorcising a demon. Now, let's continue with the exorcism."

"Okay."

Madame La Belle continued the exorcism. She sprinkled some white power on Avery. She started to recite another page from the book. She wrote some more symbols on the floor around Avery in ox blood. She started to spin and prance around Avery. She waved some burning incense. Finally, after chanting for ten minutes, she stopped. She took off the mask. Her aged face was drenched with sweat.

"I don't sense a demon in you, child."

"What do you mean?"

"I don't sense a demon in you."

"Then what is Venice?"

"Who is Venice?" Madame La Belle asked.

"My demon."

"No, child. You have no demons residing in you."

"Well give me my hundred bucks back," Hannah demanded. Madame La Belle snickered.

"I did the full exorcism. Start to finish. Now leave." She started pushing the two through the door.

Hannah and Avery didn't speak much on the drive home. Avery was wondering what she would tell her mother about the pig's blood.

Avery felt defeated and desperate. The exorcism failed miserably. She wondered what Venice would do if she found out.

Chapter Seven

The Victims

AVERY MANAGED TO SNEAK INTO THE HOUSE unnoticed and wash the pig's blood off her face and arms. She thought about Venice. What was she dealing with? The exorcism had failed which meant that Venice was not a demon.

In her room Avery found her copy of *The Silver Spoon* by Pennie Apples. Avery noticed the cashier had slipped inside a flyer regarding Pennie's book signing. Coincidently it would take place tomorrow. Avery split the book open. She smelled the fresh ink on the pages and began reading. The book was a page turner. The more Avery read, the more she grew to like this Pennie Apples. Avery forgot all about Venice as she read the book and made up her mind to go to Pennie's book signing. Soon, Avery fell asleep.

She dreamed again that night. In her dream, Avery stood on a moonlit beach. Animals could be heard in the forest bordering in the beach. The sand was warm under her toes. Suddenly, she felt something hit her shoulder. She looked around to see a round brown eyeball. She heard someone giggle in the distance. Another object hit her back: a second brown eyeball. Then she felt something really hard hit her head. Avery fell to the ground from the blow. She glanced over and saw a dog collar lying on the ground. It had a name on it: "Pooshie."

"The best part of killing the dog was the eyeballs. I kept one as a souvenir," Venice whispered in her ear.

The doorbell woke her up the next day. She shivered a little bit. No one was home so Avery hurried down the steps to answer the door in her pajamas. The next-door neighbor Mrs.

Crane stood outside. Avery quickly opened the door.

"Hello, Mrs. Crane. May I help you?" Avery asked. Mrs. Crane was wearing her bathrobe and looked very distraught. Mrs. Crane had been widowed for some time now. She was a nice elderly woman. Avery had never seen her gray hair in curlers before.

"Have you seen my dog, Pooshie?" she asked Avery.

"I have not, why? Is something wrong?" Mrs. Crane started to cry.

"He has been missing since last night! I let him out about 4pm! I shut the door and let him do his business. Now, I don't know where he is!"

"I am so sorry Mrs. Crane. What breed was he?" She sniffed and wiped her eyes on her bathrobe.

"He was a golden retriever." Avery stiffened up. A golden retriever, the same dog from her dream.

"I am sorry, Mrs. Crane. I hope you find your dog soon. I will keep an eye out for Pooshie." Avery shut the door.

Avery sat on the couch and thought about her nightmare: Venice must have been controlling her again. She thought Venice might retaliate in response to the exorcism but she had never imagined Venice would kill the neighbor's dog. Avery didn't know what she was capable of. The only thing she could think of was to see Pennie Apples. Avery couldn't go to the police station and tell them what was going on. They would think she was crazy.

Avery started yelling for Venice. She needed to know if the dog really was murdered.

"Venice, Venice, Venice!" Avery yelled.

"Over here." Avery turned to Venice sitting in the kitchen. "So, what is it you wish to ask me?" Venice asked.

"You know exactly." Avery sat down in front of her.

"I don't know. Enlighten me." Venice smiled at Avery. It reminded her of the old Venice. The malevolent one from her childhood.

"The dog named Pooshie. Where is it?" Venice let out a laugh. "You know the best part about murdering the dog? It made me feel so alive! It made me feel like for once, I wasn't stuck with you," she responded.

"I knew it was you!"

"No, actually it was you, Avery. It was you! Remember I told you we were twins. You and I, we share the same body. You can't live without me and I can't live without you!"

Avery lunged for her throat. Her hands went right through Venice. She stared in shock.

"That's right? You can't touch me. You are powerless. You are inferior to me!" Venice responded. She got up off the chair and walked away. She faded away as she walked. Avery could still hear her cruel laughter even after she was gone.

The next day Avery woke up with a throbbing headache. She swayed as she made her way to the bathroom. She vomited in the toilet bowl. After Avery threw up she stared at the spots of blood mixed in with the vomit. She lay down on the floor of the bathroom. She wondered if she had the flu.

Avery made her way to work. She sat in traffic for a while but as she drove up to the shopping center, she could see the scene was chaotic. There were news crews and police standing in front of the nail salon. Avery parked quickly and walked up to the hectic scene. She maneuvered through the cameramen and reporters. She heard Mr. Troung's voice in the crowd. Avery squeezed between a fat cameraman and a woman reporter.

"Sir, do you believe any of your employees is the murderer?" one of the reporters asked. She was a female reporter with short brown hair. She wore a blue suit and had on heavy makeup. Mr. Troung was wearing a mustard yellow cotton shirt with a pair of black pants. He was sweating so much that his glasses were fogging up.

"I don't know, all my employees are nice people. I don't know anyone who would kill these people," he answered with his broken accent.

"Sir, do you know any of the victims? Why were they naked?" a reporter asked. This reporter was a man. He had black hair and a bushy mustache.

"I don't know. I don't know. This is bad luck to my business. Now I have to get a priest to come bless the shop."

"Sir, do you believe the bodies were dumped in the dumpster by someone who wanted to act out in revenge? Maybe as a personal attack on you?"

"I don't know. I have no enemies." A heavyset cop came out of the crowd and started backing reporters out of Mr. Troung's face.

"Mr. Troung what about work?" Avery yelled. After this Avery could only see white as cameras flashed.

"An employee!" someone yelled. Reporters began bombarding her with questions.

"Do you feel your life is in danger?" a female voice asked.

"Do think someone working with you is a murderer?" a male asked.

"Are you afraid to go to work after seeing the crime scene?" a hoarse voice asked.

Avery couldn't answer. She felt a sharp tug and was swept away into a police car. Mr. Troung sat next to her. He was really pouring down sweat now. His mustard colored shirt was drenched.

"Don't say anything to those reporters," he said in Vietnamese.

"I won't. What is going on?" Avery replied in Vietnamese as well. She guessed that he didn't want the officer to listen to their conversation.

"This morning I found bodies in the dumpster behind the salon."

"Oh!" The officer began driving them to the police station. Avery assumed he was going to question her.

"Don't worry, I don't think anyone from the salon did it. I think a competitor did it to scare away customers."

"What happened? Why did they ask if I was scared?" Mr. Troung remained quiet for a minute before answering.

"The bodies were found with their eyeballs gouged out and tongues cut out. The police believe the killer took them for trophies."

"Gosh, are you okay after seeing that?"

"Yes, I worked in a slaughter house when I first came to America. I have seen much worse. The police say their genitals were mutilated with a knife as well."

"Wow," Avery said, amazed. The murders were brutal.

At the police station, Avery was questioned. Drill sergeant were the only words Avery could use to describe this detective. He spit in her face, and bombarded her with questions relating to where she had been the night before. Avery told him that she had been sleeping soundly. He finally let her go after an agonizing few minutes but the officers took a DNA sample before she left. Avery drove home, thinking about who could have killed those people.

Later on that evening Avery turned on the TV. She watched as the news anchors announced that the victims had one thing connecting them all. They all attended the same swinger's club, according to an anonymous source. Avery gulped. Her heart started beating fast. She wondered if it was Ninth Heaven.

Avery called out to Venice once again. She knew she would appear if she kept at it. Venice showed up minutes later.

"What is it?" Venice asked.

"Did you?" Venice smiled. She made herself comfortable on the couch.

"Maybe…"

"You killed those people?"

"Well, with a good reason of course."

"What is a good reason to you, Venice? Seriously! Did you do it with my body again? You know I am in big enough trouble with the dog, now people?"

"Oh stop your complaining! Those people deserved it! They, they said I couldn't be an actress! A real glamorous Hollywood celebrity! Those assholes regret ever saying that! I made them pay, pay for telling me: "You're a great fuck but you wouldn't make it in Hollywood." Venice looked psychotic.

"I wish I could get rid of you! I wish you were never here! Those people were right, you wouldn't make it in Hollywood! For Christ's sake, you're not even fucking real!" Avery said with labored breathing. She could feel a sharp pain in her back. It was getting more painful by the minute.

Venice's face was red. She glared at Avery. How dare she tell her such a thing? Venice was real, and she would show her. She would get her revenge by killing someone close to Avery.

"I *am* real, Avery. Feel that pain in your back? That's me, and I am not going away! I am going to keep murdering people, I will make sure you spend the rest of your life in prison!" Venice screamed.

Avery watched as she disappeared again. She felt relief as the pain in her back subsided.

Chapter Eight

Pennie Apples the Albino Psychic

AVERY BOUGHT HANDCUFFS AFTER HER ARGUMENT with Venice. She decided to fasten herself to the bed that night. There was no telling what Venice would do next since she had admitted to killing a dog and those people in the dumpster. Avery wondered what Venice meant by her twin. As far as she knew she had no other twin. She would have to talk to her mother about it later. She tossed the keys to unlock the handcuffs to the other side of the room. Avery was uncomfortable. She had never been handcuffed to the bed before. After some time she was able to get used to the steel around her wrists.

The next day, Avery was stuck to the bed.

"Mom, mom, mom!" Avery yelled.

"What are you yelling about?" Peter asked. He peeked in Avery's room.

"Can you please get the keys for me?" Avery pointed to the handcuff keys.

"Give me twenty bucks and I will do it." Peter grinned. Avery glared at him.

"Fine, in my purse there is twenty bucks." Peter retrieved his twenty dollars from Avery's purse.

"You want these?" Peter said teasing her with the keys. He jiggled the keys in front of her face.

"Yes, just toss them to me."

"Here." Peter tossed them on Avery's stomach.

Later that day, Avery walked through the rows of bookshelves at Barnes and Noble. She was very nervous about finally meeting Pennie Apples. Avery didn't know how to start off telling her about Venice. She still needed to figure out what ex-actly Venice was. At least she had been able to cross out demon and stillborn baby off the list.

Avery crept up silently to the book signing. She was watching carefully from behind a bookshelf. The fans standing in line were older and they looked quite normal for Pennie Apple fans. The fan who was getting his book signed was in his seventies with white hair, thick spectacles, and liver spots dotting his hands. Pennie Apples herself was different than she expected. She was an albino! She didn't even look like the women from the poster. Her hair was white as a seagull's feather. Her skin was almost translucent. Her eyes were pink. It was strange. Avery had never seen an albino person up close before. She was wearing a professional but sleek black dress with black high heels and black-rimmed glasses.

"Are you here for the book signing, young lady?" Avery turned around to see a very tall Hispanic lady. She was looking sharp in a soft navy blue business suit. She wore modest navy blue flats. She quickly tried to think of something clever to say but came up short.

"I'm here for the book signing."

"Do you have your copy of *The Silver Spoon*?"

"Yes," Avery said, nervously holding her copy of the book.

"What is your name?" the women demanded.

"My name is Avery Tran."

"My name is Stacy Orta. Nice to meet you."

"Nice to meet you as well." The woman turned and walked to the table to stand beside Pennie Apples. Avery guessed she must be her agent or worked for the publishing company. Pennie Apples turned to look at Avery from behind the table and their eyes locked. Her pink eyes narrowed looking her up and down. Then she gave her a big smile, which Avery returned. She turned back to the man in the nice suit. He was talking a mile a minute. He was obviously infatuated by her. Avery continued to sip on her green tea Frappuccino and wait-ed in line quietly.

"So what did you think of the book?" a teenage boy whis-pered from behind her. He had crazy hair. It was brown with blond highlights and spiked up with gel. His eyes were dark brown. His shirt had a stick figure stabbing itself. It's a shirt that Avery could see at Hot Topic.

"It was pretty good, what did you think?"

"I loved that her most famous case was finding a kidnapped CIA agent from Virginia all the way in Bangkok, Thailand. I liked the part where the guy was found hung upside down with women's panties in his mouth and his hands were tied behind his back. There was also the case of the kidnapped daughter of a Mexican drug kingpin. She was raped and strangled to death just like Pennie said she would be. The father didn't believe her till they found his daughter's body."

"I liked the one with the bank robbers because Pennie caught them only one day after the robbery. They didn't even get to spend the three million euros they stole from the bank in Rome. They thought they would get away with it but Pennie led the police to their hideout."

"I know, it's great isn't it? Pennie is my hero!" the boy swooned. He was smitten by her.

"Don't forget the art thief case. The guy was renowned in the underground criminal world for forging paintings that he stole. The guy ended up stealing this expensive painting from some Brazilian billionaire. The billionaire didn't even notice until Pennie Apples notified him. He is very thankful for her. She gave them the location of the thief," Avery said.

"Yeah, that art thief was pretty clever but not clever enough," the boy said.

"Pretty crazy. I really like Pennie,"

After a short wait it was finally her turn to speak to "The Renowned Pennie Apples." She looked at Avery with her pink eyes from behind those square glasses. Avery was mesmerized by how beautiful she was. She must have been at least in her late thirties. Her white hair was wavy around her shoulders. Her skin was white as cream but had a soft texture to it. The black dress she wore made her skin look deathly white. Those pink eyes were just so intense. Avery felt like they were peering into her soul. She was intimidated and couldn't speak. Pennie was the first one to say something.

"The copy of your book please?" She pushed up her glasses and got her sharpie ready. Avery gave her the book.

"Your name please sweetie?" Avery snapped back to reality.

"My name…My name…is Avery Tran." Avery stuttered a bit. She could feel herself blushing immensely.

"That is a very pretty name, Avery. Would you like me to write anything special on the book for you?" Those pink eyes really made her uneasy.

"Well. I am a big fan of those cases of yours. You know the one involving missing people. I know you work with cases like that a lot. The art theft involving that Brazilian billionaire was fascinating." Avery talked quickly.

"I am glad you have been following me. So what do you do, Avery?" She was writing a very long message on the book.

"Right now, I am a college student working part time in a nail salon."

"Fascinating. It wouldn't happen to be the nail salon on TV, would it?"

"It is, the one where they found those bodies."

"Wow, you have to tell me everything about you, Avery. How about we talk after I read my chapter from the book?"

"Sure," Avery said, coolly. Pennie finished autographing her book. She handed it back to her. Their fingers touched briefly. Avery felt an electric shock between them. Evidently so did Pennie Apples. She looked surprised, then coughed and straightened herself out.

Avery headed over to the sci fi section of Barnes and Nobles. The employees had cleared out the bookshelves with some cozy chairs and couches. All of Pennie's fans were holding their copies of *Silver Spoon*. An Indian lady was sitting on an easy chair and two heavy set black women were gossiping away on the loveseat next to her. A South American man was sitting next to Avery. He was wearing a grey business suit. He looked to be in his late twenties. His hair was golden wavy and the color of hay. It came down to his shoulders. His eyes were brown. He glanced over at her copy of the book.

"What did she write on your copy?" He sounded like he

was Argentinian or Brazilian. She glanced down at the book and opened the front page. Avery saw what Pennie Apples scribbled on the page. To Avery's surprise this is what she wrote.

For Miss Avery Tran,

It was nice to meet you. Remember to do your homework, and communicate with your professors. I also have to say: anyone who comes to my book signing wearing that adorable canary yellow halter top and velvety pants to match is a friend of mine. You are an intriguing young lady.

Dream big and look to the skies,

Pennie Apples

Avery showed the man this. He smiled.

"She must have really liked you. Amazing you can make an impression in a few minutes."

"I showed you mine now you show me yours," Avery retorted. He brushed back his wavy long hair.

"Look away Miss. Avery Tran." He emphasized her name. His accent was alluring. Avery loved his minty fresh breath. Avery looked down at his copy of the book. Scribbled away at the front was this.

For Mr. Rafael Costa,

You sound passionate about my work. I am happy to meet such a big fan!

Dream big and look to the skies,

Pennie Apples

"She likes you, Mr. Costa," Avery said, handing the book back to Rafael. He reminded Avery of handsome surfer guys but in a suit.

"It's Rafael. Please call me Rafael. Miss Apples likes me because I am arm candy…"

"Well, you can't blame her now can you, Rafael?"

"What are you doing today, Avery?"

"Well I am here for the book signing and reading, but afterwards I really don't know what I am going to do." Rafael gave her a mischievous smile. Pennie Apples took the floor. Everyone was quieting down.

"Please give me your number so we can get together later," he whispered to her, handing Avery his phone. She typed in the number.

"Alright Avery, I will call you later?"

"Please." Avery spoke with her most charming voice.

Pennie Apples began to read the first chapter of her book. It was interesting how it started out from the perspective of the character looking back on her childhood. Avery was taken aback when she mentioned her character had been a medium who could see ghosts in her childhood. She must be a very spiritual person. She mentioned that she had been abused by her siblings and classmates for being "special." It fascinated Avery how Pennie had grown up poor and living in the projects of New York City. She also talked about how her German family had migrated to the country and worked in a sweatshop. She worked with them. It was a terrible ordeal for her. She seemed so real this Pennie Apples.

"Thank you all for coming to my book signing and reading. If you have any questions or comments come up and speak with me." A flood of her fans went to the table she had been sitting on while doing the book reading.

"Would you like to get some lunch next door? There is a Cheesecake Factory," Rafael asked her.

"Another time, Rafael. You have my number. Call me if you need me." He stood and took her hand. Rafael kissed Avery's hand. His lips were so soft and supple.

"It was great meeting you here of all places. I will call or text you soon." He left with a swift swish.

Avery looked over to see that Pennie was still being mobbed by fans. She waited quietly until all the fans were done talking to her. Pennie strutted over.

"So tell me more about this nail salon." Pennie sat down on the couch beside her.

"Well, my boss is very rude, he wears huge thick glasses, and looks like a pedophile." Pennie laughed.

"No, darling. Tell me about the murders."

"Well, my boss told me they were brutally murdered. All my boss told me was the victims' genitals were mutilated."

"Sounds like a cult killing," Pennie said, her pink eyes making Avery nervous.

"Maybe."

"Did you feel it?" Pennie asked, changing the subject.

"Feel what?"

"Feel that jolt between us." Avery looked down and away.

"Yes…"

"I feel there is something off about you."

"Oh, come on, you're doing the whole cheesy psychic thing? Really?"

"Yeah, sure, why not?"

"Well, now that you mention it, there is something wrong." Avery went on to tell Pennie about Venice. Pennie didn't make a comment when Avery mentioned she was an imaginary friend. She went on to talk about Venice's harassment. Avery told her about the attempts to discard Venice, doing the blotched exorcism and digging up the stillborn. Now Venice was angry after Avery's failed attempts to discard her. She even confessed to murdering innocent victims. This was her retaliation against Avery. She even told Pennie how Venice said she would put Avery in jail.

"Wow, I can't believe it," Pennie said after Avery told her story.

"I know, Venice used to be my friend. Now, she is ruining my life. I mean she confessed, and told me I am going to prison."

"So do you know for sure if you murdered those innocent people?" Pennie inquired.

"Venice told me."

"You mentioned she said she was your twin? The police

officers hasn't come and arrested you. Why do you believe this Venice?" Pennie asked.

"My neighbor Mrs. Crane was trying to find her dog. I had a dream about the dog being murdered the night before. Venice confessed to killing the dog. What other proof do I need? I am so worried, I handcuffed myself to the bed."

"You know, why we don't go see this stillborn's grave. I am curious, maybe this Venice is the ghost of the stillborn. Maybe the stillborn is your twin Venice."

"Maybe."

"Let me talk to my agent over there." Pennie walked over to her agent and talked for a few minutes. She smiled at Avery walking back.

"Well, my agent said it was okay to go with you. Joe, my bodyguard, will be following us. This was the only way Stacy would agree with this." Pennie nodded to Joe. He was standing by Stacy. He had an enormous figure. He was not only tall but very muscular. His head was completely shaven and he wore a dark suit with even darker sunglasses.

"Okay, so what car are we taking?" Avery asked.

"Yours, let's get this over with. Find out what Venice really is."

In the car, Avery was quiet for the first few moments. She didn't know what to say. She didn't know if going back to the stillborn would be a good idea. What would Venice do next? Avery was glad she purchased the handcuffs.

"Tell me more about this imaginary friend of yours,"

"Well she has been with me for as long as I can remember. She always wears the most ridiculous outfits."

"What race is she?" Pennie asked.

"She is Asian," Avery said quietly. She wondered where Pennie was going with this.

"Oh I see, Asian, so you believe she is actual the ghost of your dead sibling?

"I don't know. We had an exorcism and everything. I don't know if it worked."

"What was the exorcism like?"

"It was a little scary. My friend Hannah and I found the

woman who performed the exorcism on craigslist. Her name was Madame La Belle. She put pig's blood on me. She danced around with a tribal mask. She chanted the entire time in a foreign language I couldn't understand."

"Sounds like a shaman."

"I was thinking she was one. She told us at the end of the exorcism that I didn't have a demon inside me."

"This is when you ruled out the possibility of Venice being a demon?"

"Yes."

"So have you seen Venice since the exorcism?"

"Yes, when the murders happened. I knew she had to be the culprit. She told me she possesses me at night. She wants me to go to prison. I don't know why she is so angry. I assume it is because she knows I was trying to get rid of her."

"What a startling confession for an imaginary friend. I guess we will soon find out what she is."

They were getting close to the gravesite now. Avery was starting to get aches all over her body. The closer they got to the grave the more Avery felt dizzy. Suddenly she could feel a sinister presence in the backseat. She kept looking in the review mirror but nothing was sitting back there. Her intuition told her that Venice was back there, however, seething with anger about the situation.

The park was coming into view. Pennie seemed to be at the very edge of her seat. After talking with Avery. She had a good idea what Venice was. She had read a case about it many years ago.

Avery pulled into a parking space. The park was empty for a Saturday afternoon. On the way over, she had seen dark clouds forming and the wind was picking up. A storm was coming. Joe parked next to them in the large black SUV.

"Okay, we are here." Pennie got out of the car and gave the park a once over.

"This isn't a bad place to bury a miscarriage…"

"Follow me, Pennie."

"This is such a quiet park. What a nice resting place for someone." They passed the playground where the children play. The swings were swaying in the wind. Avery couldn't shake the feeling that Venice was following them. She kept looking behind to see if Venice would pop up.

Avery looked behind her to see Joe following them. Having him following behind them gave her a sense of comfort. Pennie and Avery walked in silence toward the remote back of the park where she had buried the miscarriage. The trees became thick as they stepped off the walking trail. Avery felt the hairs on her arms rise up. This ominous feeling was not going away. Pennie suddenly grabbed her hand. She smiled at Avery like a mother would smile at a newborn baby.

"Don't be scared Avery. You have me and Joe is right behind us." Avery squeezed her hand. They kept walking. Pennie was not having as hard a time walking through the terrain in high heels. She moved with grace and poise. Her long white hair swirled around her in the wind. Her pink eyes were mysterious. She looked mystical and out of this world. They approached the gravesite with caution.

"Is this it?" Pennie was looking at the pink cross Avery had laid down on the grave.

"Yes, do you feel anything?" Pennie looked disappointed.

"No, darling, if there was a soul here, it's long gone. I wish I could be more helpful. Though there is something that might help." Pennie looked behind her. Joe walked up with a black bag.

"I thought you might need this just in case Miss Apples." He handed Pennie the bag with ease.

"Are you ready, Avery? This substance is illegal in the US. I got it from Sweden. It heightens my senses and gives me more insight." Pennie took a small green flask from Joe. She poured a little of substance out of the bottle into the glass that Joe was holding. The wind had calmed down a little.

"What is that, Pennie?" Avery asked.

"It's absinthe. It helps me connect with nature and spirits."

"I've never heard of it before." Pennie put a silver spoon on the wine glass. Joe checked his suit pocket. He pulled out a sugar cube. Pennie put the sugar cube on the spoon.

"You have never heard of it before because my darling it

was illegal in the US a long time ago. This is very important now. I must concentrate on pouring a slow steady stream onto the cube." Avery wondered why it was illegal. How was she able to get it over here? What does it do to you really? Joe supplied the answer.

"It's illegal because it causes seizures and all types of medical problems along with hallucinations. It is at least seventy percent alcohol. This one however only has fifty percent alcohol. I made sure of that when I bought it." Pennie glared at Joe.

"I wanted the seventy percent, Joe! How will I be able to work under these conditions? I can't even trust you to get me absinthe!"

"You will thank me later, Pennie. You know I'm very worried about you." Pennie pushed up her glasses and began to pour the water from the water bottle into a glass pitcher.

"We should get this over with. Poor Avery needs to know who this Venice entity is. This is a good place to start."

Pennie poured a little bit of the water onto the sugar cube, just enough to soak it. Then she continued to pour a steady stream of water onto the cube dissolving it slowly. It was like nothing Avery ever saw before. Here they were in the middle of the park. This illegal drink was being prepared right before her eyes. The sugar cube finally melted as the water filled up the glass. The dark green liquid had turned a light green color. Pennie took a real spoon and stirred the concoction.

"And there you have it. Good old-fashioned absinthe." She held up the glass. Avery watched her slowly take a sip of the green liquid.

"Oh delightful! You must try one sip, Avery." Her curiosity about the drink got the better of her. Pennie handed her the glass. Avery looked at it cautiously. Pennie spoke up.

"Go ahead and drink it, dear. Don't be afraid. Let the herbal taste arouse your virgin tongue. Just a sip though. Not too much. I must have you drink a sip. It is part of my ritual." Avery saw Joe shaking his head in the background. She took a sip. It burned her tongue and tasted horrible. It tasted like black licorice. It was not an herbal flavor like Pennie described at all. Joe rushed over. He took the glass from her hands. She rolled over on the grass and grabbed her stomach. Avery coughed and coughed. Pennie patted her back.

"You took a big gulp dear. What did you think was going to happen?" Avery rolled her eyes. Her throat burned. Taking deep breaths, she finally stopped coughing. Pennie stood up.

"On with the ritual." She took the glass from Joe again. She drank the glass down slowly. She looked a little tipsy.

Joe handed her another item from the bag. It was a bundle of dried herbs. Pennie called it a smudge stick. The stick was bundled together with sage, rosemary, or some other herbs. Pennie grabbed the smudge stick and lit it with a lighter. She kneeled before the miscarriage grave. She let ashes from the burning smudge stick fall into a metal bowl full of sand before her. Pennie threw her hands up and started to chant in foreign language. During the ritual she shook the smudge stick at times. Pennie chanted louder and louder. Avery heard the sound of a baby crying. The trees swayed. Pennie stopped chanting and waving her hands. She took a deep breath. She was sweating profusely.

"The miscarriage is gone. I don't sense any anger here." She said all this with labored breathing. Avery leaned over to help her up. Pennie took her hand. Almost immediately she fell back on the ground and started speaking in tongues. Joe came over. He slapped her once but not hard. He used what was left in the water bottle to awaken Pennie. He poured some water on his hands and touched her face gently with his saturated hand. Pennie snapped back to reality.

"Oh Avery! It was horrible. There is something inside of you. Something sick and twisted." Avery kicked the dirt.

"I know that already. It's Venice, right?" Pennie stood up and drank the rest of what was in the water bottle.

"It was just so malevolent." Joe had her in his arms. He was patting her back.

"So did you see Venice when you touched me?" Avery asked. Pennie looked at her with big pink eyes.

"It was your twin. All I know is that the thing is angry and wants out." Joe helped her up off the ground.

"Thanks for all your help," Avery said, disappointed. All her hopes were let down when Pennie mentioned the word twin. "I already know Venice is my twin. I came to you to figure out how to get rid of her."

"This place gives me the creeps. Let's get out of here." Joe put everything in the bag. He put it down on the ground. Joe took out a flashlight from inside his suit pocket. He handed it to her.

After riding home in the rain by herself, Avery lit a smudge stick at home that Pennie had given her. She said it would cleanse the house of negative energies. Pennie also gave her personal phone number to Avery. The smoke alarm went off.

"What are you doing in here?" Her mother asked barging into the room. Avery quickly quieted the fire alarm.

"Nothing, mother."

"What's that in your hand? Why are your burning things in your room? What is going on?"

"Nothing is going on." Muoi looked suspicious. She put her hands on her hips.

"You better not be doing anything nefarious. You are good girl. Don't be like your sister Anna. Go to school, and get a well-paying job. That's all I ever wanted for you."

"Okay, mother. Please go now. I need to rest." Avery pushed her mother out of the room.

Chapter Nine

Venice's Retaliation

PENNIE AND JOE MADE THEIR WAY BACK to the Hilton in Arlington. Pennie braced herself before she opened the hotel room door. Joe had left her alone after returning to his own room. She knew Stacy was going to scold her for being out later than she expected. She entered the room. Stacy was waiting for Pennie on the couch in the living room area. Pennie took off her wedges before stepping onto the white carpet. Stacy's face was red with rage. Her dark hair was placed in a neat bun and she was wearing another silk black business suit. Stacy's beautiful brown Hispanic eyes followed Pennie as she sat down on the easy chair in front of her. Stacy was the first one to talk.

"Do you have anything smart to say?" Stacy asked. She sounded calm enough but her face said it all.

"Well, as matter of fact, I have a new book idea. I am going to write soon." Stacy lightened up a bit.

"So you have a new book idea. Enlighten me." Pennie blew out softly.

"Well, it's about a young girl who has an unequally conjoined twin inside her."

"Care to elaborate on that?" Stacy raised her perfectly tweezed eyebrow.

"When I was with Avery, I touched her and I saw the parasitic twin. It was a huge brain attached to her spinal cord. I believe it is gaining control of her body. I am planning on writing a book about it."

"Why is this Avery girl so important to you? Why is she so special?" Stacy asked.

"Stacy have you been following along with what I just said? At all? She is the girl with the parasitic twin inside her."

"Ah, I see, so what are you going to do?"

"Well, I have done some research on parasitic twins before."

"And what did you find?"

"Well it is sort of hard to explain. I will let you read some articles that I looked up." Pennie handed Stacy her sleek Macbook Air.

Stacy began to read the first article about parasitic twins. A man from India had a parasitic twin growing inside his stomach. He lived with it for about forty-five years until it started causing him pain. He spent about eight hours in the hospital for surgery. The surgeon who worked on him was surprised to find the parasitic twin. The man was stunned as well: the twin weighed a staggering forty pounds. After the surgery the man brought the twin back to the village and buried it. He gave it a proper Indian burial.

The second article Stacy read was the most interesting. This story happened recently in the state of Hawaii. The woman with the parasitic twin was married and worked with her husband in a sushi restaurant. She was Japanese and so was her husband. The woman complained about having riveting nightmares and sleepwalking while the twin was inside her. Then one night her husband found her in the kitchen chopping up a fish with a large knife. Her husband said she looked completely different, like she had been possessed or something. She lunged at him with the large butcher knife. He in self-defense grabbed the frying pan and whacked her on the head. She fell to the floor unconscious. The husband called the local police and retold his story to them. He loved his wife, but he knew what he saw in the kitchen that night wasn't her. They released his wife since he didn't want to press charges. He took her home and they had a CAT scan done to look inside her. The doctors discovered that she had a parasitic twin growing in her brain. They immediately scheduled surgery to take it out and the husband had to lock up his own wife until it was completed because the unequally conjoined twin was trying to kill him. The doctors operated on the woman for several hours. They finally got the twin out without killing her. The twin was a half-pound brain and some skin. The brain died almost immediately after being removed but the surgeons said that if it had been any bigger, it would have killed the poor woman, or worse, taken over her body. It was amazing this story hadn't made it to national news.

"I understand now, has Avery's twin started murdering people yet?" Stacy inquired.

"According to Avery the twin has manifested itself in front of her as an imaginary friend. She names herself Venice. Venice has confessed to murdering the victims found in the dumpster of Beautiful Nails. She also confessed to murdering a neighbor's dog."

"Oh, so Avery will be going to jail then?"

"I don't think so. I have a plan."

"Venice confessed to committing the crimes. She must have been able to control Avery's body."

"Yes, Avery did mention this. She said Venice controls her at night. Take in consideration this is what her twin is telling her."

"So what are you going to do?"

"I do not know yet. I want to write a book about this. We need physical proof that Avery's twin killed those swingers."

"Does Avery know about this twin?"

"Well, Avery doesn't know she has an asymmetrical twin. I have to inform her soon. I just didn't want to shock her right away. The poor girl, she is so innocent. I need to also get a CAT scan performed on her and a neurologist to look at her."

"Well, it sounds like you have a lot of work to do." Pennie's stomach growled.

"Why don't we get dinner?" Stacy asked.

"It is late but I am sure we can still order room service."

"Sounds good. I am starving too."

Back at Avery's house, she had a restful night's sleep, assisted by the smudging she had done earlier. She yawned and stretched. It took her a moment to realize the handcuffs were off of her. What happened last night? What did she do? What did Venice do? Avery sat up, and pulled the cover to her chin.

She was afraid to venture out of the room. The house was quiet.

"Would you like me to tell you what happened last night?" Venice had appeared at the foot of Avery's bed. Her black hair was tangled and messy. She wore a strait jacket. Venice's smile was crooked and her eyes were crossed.

"What did you do Venice?"

"Nothing…"

"What did you do?" Venice faced Avery and gave her a cruel smile.

"I killed her." Avery's jaw dropped.

"Who did you kill, Venice? Who did you kill?"

"Our mother!" Venice let out a barbaric laugh. She kicked her feet and danced around joyfully. "Our mother is dead! The bitch is finally dead! I waited years and years!" Avery ran from the room into her mother's bedroom.

"No!!!!" Avery cried.

Her mother was lying in bed face down with bloody sheets surrounding her. Avery grabbed her black hair and sank down beside of her mother. No, no, how could she? How could Venice kill her mother? Tears streamed down Avery's face.

"She tried to get rid of me you know!" Venice said sitting down beside Avery.

"What? What are you talking about Venice?"

"When you were born! She had the doctor remove part of me."

"What? What are you talking about?"

"She tried to get rid of me! She tried to get rid of her own daughter! Not just her, though, our father too. The drunk bastard went along with the idea of surgery!"

"You are fucking evil! That's why she got rid of you! You're a bitch! You killed your own mother, Venice!" Avery wiped tears from her eyes and continued to hug her mother's dead body. The ache in her back was searing, but she knew she had to suppress Venice at some point.

"I am not! I am Venice! I am powerful. I tricked Muoi. She came when she heard me calling her name. She flipped when she saw you handcuffed to the bed. So Muoi uncuffed me and I slit her throat! Yes, I killed a mother who did not accept me! I killed her and now she is gone! I'll kill you next Avery!"

Avery had had enough of Venice. She sat and stared at her, contemplating what to do next.

"Get back inside! You need to go somewhere else for a while. I don't want you around!"

"No, no, NO!" Venice cried. Black chains wrapped around her. She struggled against the chains.

"Go back to where you came from!" Avery said louder. The black chains tightened around Venice.

"I'll be back! I will kill everyone you love!" Venice said before disappearing.

Avery sat in her mother's bed for a long time. She cradled her mother's dead body fondly. She mourned and mourned. Her heart ached, and she felt weak. Avery dragged herself out of her mother's bed. She picked up the phone and dialed 911.

"Hello this is 911. What is your emergency today?"

"My mother is dead," Avery managed to say.

"Your mother is dead?"

"Yes, I have checked her pulse. She is dead."

"We are sending emergency vehicles and police officers," the woman on the other line said calmly.

"Thank you." Avery hung up. She dialed Pennie's number next.

Avery sat on the bed waiting for Pennie to pick up her phone. Finally she did pick up.

"Hello?"

"Pennie, its Avery! Venice, she… she killed my mother."

"What? What is going on?"

"Pennie, I am turning myself in. Can you get me a good lawyer who can prove Venice did this?"

"Yes, yes of course. Honey, are you okay?"

"I don't know," Avery said. The tears started falling down her face again. She wiped them up as fast as they fell. Avery heard a knock on the door. She went downstairs to see the paramedics, police officers, and firemen had arrived.

"I have to go, Pennie," Avery said before hanging up the phone.

The police officers took a look at Muoi Tran. The crime scene investigators were called. Avery was still crying and emotional. The officers tried talking to her but all she could do was squeak. After a while, they were able to convince her to go to headquarters and talk.

The light in the interrogation room was dim. An officer sat across Avery. He stared at her intently. Avery took a sip of her coffee. It tasted awful like motor oil. She swallowed it.

"So Avery, why is it you were covered in Muoi's blood?" he asked.

"I was trying to revive her."

"So you didn't kill her?" The man asked. Venice started talking to Avery internally.

(Don't you say anything to him, Avery.)(Venice, what are you doing inside my head?)(I am here to stay, I told you so. Don't you tell him, you killed your mother.)(If they were smart they would find out anyways.)(Avery, you better not tell. I have plans for us.)(Plans for you.)(Darling, don't you want to live a fabulous life? Don't you want to be a renowned actress in Hollywood?)(No, I want my mother back.) Venice took a moment to respond. (Well, she is dead. Gone, baby, gone. She was holding you back.)(What? She wasn't holding me back. I hope you die. You don't deserve to live. Go back where you came from, you aren't welcome in my head or my body. Go!) Venice was gone. Avery contemplated her next move.

"Avery, did you kill your mother?" The officer interrupted her thoughts.

"My twin killed her, officer."

"Who is your twin? Where is she? What is her name?" the officer persisted.

"Her name is Venice. She says she is part of me."

"So you killed your mother?"

"Not exactly," Avery said vaguely.

Pennie drove to Lorenzo Fernandez's law firm. She didn't know what was going on with Avery. All she knew was that Avery would need a good lawyer. The law firm was immaculately clean. Not a spot of dirt on the nice white marble tile. A shark tank was positioned behind the receptionist's desk. The hammerheads, bull, and tiger sharks swam lazily in their enormous tank.

Pennie stepped into Lorenzo's office, which took up an entire floor. His receptionist sat at her black desk chatting on the phone. She had her blond hair in a bun.

"May I help you?" the receptionist asked.

"Yes, I am here for Lorenzo Fernandez." The receptionist pushed the income button with a French manicured finger.

"Mr. Fernandez, there is a—" She paused. "Your name, please?"

"Pennie, Pennie Apples."

"Sir, there is a Pennie Apples here to see you."

"Let her in, Kimberly."

Across the room the black door swung open. A sleekly dressed man wearing grey glasses emerged. His hair was brown with grey streaks in it. His soft hazel eyes stared at her in disbelief. Pennie had almost forgot what her former lover had looked like. Seeing him again brought back painful memories.

"Well, Pennie Apples, I can't believe it is you!" he said, walking over and giving her a warm embrace.

"Hello, Lorenzo. I am here strictly for business," Pennie said.

"Oh." Lorenzo's cheerful face changed. "Well, come in, doll. What exactly do you need?"

"I'm afraid my friend Avery Tran has got herself in a bit of a shuffle. I was wondering if you could represent her."

"Is she being indicted yet?"

"No, but she will be though. I am sure of it."

"Well, if there is no trial, why does this Avery need me?"

"Oh, it is a long story, Lorenzo. I mean she just called me a while ago, saying her mother was murdered. Avery said she is turning herself in."

"If I am going to be her lawyer, I need to be there."

The officer was becoming increasingly frustrated with Avery. She wasn't responding to his questions the way he wanted her too. This girl was talking in circles. All he needed her to do was say yes, I did kill my mother.

"Avery, all I am asking you is did you murder your mother,

Muoi?"

"I don't know."

"You said before: "Not exactly." What did you mean?"

"I don't know." The door creaked open and the sergeant stuck his head in.

"Detective Bells, let the girl go. Her lawyer is here."

"Alright, sir." Avery stood up.

"Yes, Lorenzo Fernandez. He is waiting for you in the lobby," the sergeant said, letting Avery pass him.

She walked down the dimly lit hallway. She saw Pennie standing next to a Hispanic man. He was quite tall.

"Pennie! You came!" Avery squealed.

"Yes, dear. Of course, I came."

"I am glad you didn't confess to anything," Lorenzo whispered in her ear.

"But it was me," Avery whispered back.

"The DNA evidence came back! We are locking her up. Avery Tran you have the right to remain silent, anything you say will be used against you in court." The detective who had been questioning Avery cuffed her.

"On what grounds are you arresting my client?" Lorenzo asked.

"She is being charged with murdering her mother Muoi Tran."

"Avery, don't worry, I am going to get you out as soon as possible." Avery started to cry hysterically again.

"It was Venice, who did it! Not me, Venice!"

The following days dragged on. Avery was locked up in jail while Lorenzo was trying to sort things out. Avery was indicted for murdering her mother Muoi Tran, and the people from the swingers club. Lorenzo decided to go with a plea of not guilty by reason of insanity.

"I can't believe, Avery has a parasitic twin inside her, Pennie. It is just so hard for me to believe."

"That is why I say we do a CAT scan Lorenzo."

"Well, I can schedule it. I can't believe that the prosecutor was able to get her indicted. That grand jury wasn't even given all the evidence."

"Do you know anyone who will be able to perform the CAT scan?"

"I know one person: Barton Faulk, an old friend. I will have to discuss this with the district attorney and see if he will allow it."

"And if he doesn't?"

"Then, there is no hope for Avery. We need photographic evidence of the twin to present in court."

Chapter Ten

The Cerebrum

THE OFFICERS OPENED THE DOOR of the police station. Avery was mobbed by reporters and angry relatives of the deceased from Ninth Heaven. Protestors huddled behind the barricade. They held up signs that said, "The bitch killed my son. She should die by electrocution!" Another sign said, "Avery Tran should be sentenced to the death penalty!" Another picket sign being held up by an overweight mother said, "Straight to the chair with her!" These were the nicer signs. The reporters rushed in to ask questions. The first was a chubby reporter. He had a handle bar mustache and was elderly.

"Why did you do it?" he asked her, holding the microphone up to her mouth. Avery said nothing.

"Did you know the victims personally?" another asked. The flashes from the cameras made Avery dizzy. The DA stepped in front of her.

"Nothing to see here, folks. Just let the women breathe." Avery made her way through the crowd.

"Why did you mutilate their genitals? Was it a sex game gone bad?" Avery heard yet another reporter asked.

She was glad to be in the refuge of the SUV. Avery's hands were cuffed behind her back. She promised to herself if she ever got out of this alive. Avery would destroy Venice.

"Are you okay, Avery?" Lorenzo asked.

"I could be worse. I wish I would have known about Venice sooner. Then I could have destroyed her."

"I don't know, Avery. From my own knowledge, Venice is a part of you. Who knows—if you destroy her, you may end up destroying yourself."

"I want to be normal. I want to be free from Venice. From all this trouble she has caused."

"I suppose this is as good a time as any to tell you."

"Tell me what?"

"We need photographic evidence of Venice. I have scheduled a CAT scan for you."

"A CAT scan?"

"Yes, this won't be a problem will it?" Lorenzo touched Avery with his broad dark hands.

"No, when is the CAT scan going to take place?" Avery brushed off his hand. It made her unconformable. Lorenzo realized he may have gone too far. He let her be.

"I will pick you up tomorrow. Also, take note, Pennie will be in the room, when they strip you of your clothes."

"Will I be able to talk with her?"

"I don't know, you should be happy Pennie will be supervising. I really went out of my way to make it happen."

After the short drive, Avery saw it. The Dallas county jail was a tall grey building with many windows. Avery expected it to be more reinforced, with guard towers and barbed wire fencing. The SUV drove right up to the building and parked.

Inside the jail, Avery was stripped and given new prison garments. She felt exposed and vulnerable. It was embarrassing. The prison warden had even come to watch. She introduced herself as Lucile Black. Pennie watched the spectacle from afar. She was allowed to talk to Avery for five minutes.

"I should warn you. Lorenzo had them put up a security camera in your cell for safety, and because he wants to monitor you at night. It's for evidence as well. We want to see what Venice does." Avery was infuriated.

"It's an invasion of my privacy!"

"It is for evidence of Venice."

"I feel like a science experiment."

"Avery, we are trying our best to make you comfortable. We need more evidence of Venice."

"I wish I could kill Venice."

"You may end up killing yourself."

"Maybe, I want to."

"Don't say that! Avery you're young, you've barely started living."

"Your time is up," Lucile Black said marching into the room.

Pennie gave Avery a quick hug. The prison warden took Avery to her cell. Once Avery saw where she would be housed for the next couple of days, weeks, or months, she hung her head. The prison was like the ones she had seen in movies. The bars were made of steel. There was a woman in one of the cells who was unhinged and did not have a grip on reality. She looked at Avery and started speaking gibberish.

"Ignore her, she always does that," the prison warden said. They walked to the end of the hall. Avery's cell was grey and boring. The first thing Avery noticed was the bedpost and table. The legs of both were wrapped in pieces of cloth.

"This prison cell was designed just for you, doll. Look up and smile at the camera," the prison warden said. Avery looked up at the camera. It was a black camera, like the ones that you see in a convenience store.

"Is that camera on?"

"Of course it is, dear." The prison warden pushed her into the cell.

"You should be happy with this cell. It is like a luxury villa," the prison warden said. She cackled merrily. Avery observed her walking away. The guard who was with Lucile shut off the lights.

"Lights out!" she yelled. Her deep voice echoed through the hall and cells. There was an eerie silence in the cell block.

Avery could only see a little bit of her cell now. The moonlight came through the window and left horizontal shapes on the furniture. Avery grabbed the cold metal bars. She felt alone and forgotten. As she turned towards the bed, she noticed a black reading lamp on the table. She turned it on. Did the other prisoners get a reading lamp too or was it just her? She looked at the book collection on the desk. They had given her the Harry Potter series to read. Avery was tempted to read one. Instead, she turned off the reading light and crawled into the bed.

It was uncomfortable and itchy. The blanket and pillow were thin and smelly, and the mattress was not even padded. This was no luxury jail cell. Avery heard a giggle.

"Hello, sis!" Venice cooed. She sat on the end of Avery's bed. Avery could only see her silhouette through the sliver of moonlight in the cell.

"Venice, you better leave. I am not in the mood."

"Do you feel degraded and unclean after they stripped you of your civilian clothing and gave you the prison garments?"

"It's your fault, you killed my mother and those people from Ninth Heaven. I wouldn't be here if it wasn't for you."

"I propose a deal."

"What deal?"

"Well, when I was possessing your body, I researched doctors. I found one willing to remove me from your body. It is very risky but he has been practicing."

"What, no way!"

"Come on, don't you want to take this deal?"

"Venice, look around you. We are in jail!"

"I could probably break us out."

"Even if you could I wouldn't take the deal. You are dangerous to the public. I will have none of it."

"I am not dangerous. I am misunderstood."

"You killed my mother. You slit her throat!" Venice's hand slammed down on the bed.

"She was my mother too. She didn't accept me! She didn't love me! She waned to get rid of me!"

"She knew that you were a big pain in the rear! You're a murderer, and you won't change. You never will. You need to be locked away from the public. Even if it means I must be locked up too!"

"How dare you!" Venice screamed.

"How dare you kill Muoi!" Avery retorted. She lay down in the cot, ignoring Venice.

"I'll be back, I'll kill you." Venice whispered in her ear.

"You can't. We are connected. You would die if you tried to kill me."

After some time, Avery was able to sleep. Her body was

awakened and taken by Venice. She made rude gestures at the camera. She walked around the cell and bared Avery's teeth. She really wanted out of Avery's body. Venice wanted to escape to Hollywood and become a world famous actress. She knew Avery didn't share this vision with her. She would have to convince the jury of her own dreams, and her own values. It was hard for Venice to be confined with no freedom.

Avery woke up to the loud screech of the prison's cell block metal door creaking open. She heard footsteps in the distance. Avery was blinded by the sunrise. She looked up to see the prison warden Lucile Black and the guard. The guard was an obese lady. You could see her fat rolls through her uniform.

"Avery, would you come over here to the door," Lucile Black said sweetly. Avery walked over to the door and put her hands behind her back. The prison guard cuffed her. She stepped back and the cell door was opened.

"I see you already knew about the position. How did you know what to do?" the prison warden commented.

"I've seen movies," Avery responded.

"You kids and your movies. Your generation is abominable!" the prison warden said, escorting her through the cell block. Avery didn't look at any of the inmates today.

"Did the movies tell you, you can't get away with murder?" the obese prison guard asked her.

"I know I can't get away with murder." The prison guard laughed. She sounded like a man. Lucile laughed weakly.

"You sure seem like one." Avery walked on with the pair. She was nervous about pleading in front of the judge. She wondered if Venice was getting smarter and stronger. Maybe it was a good idea that they had Avery locked up. Who could she harm? The pair escorted her to a quiet part of the prison. It had no windows. It was made of concrete and had bad lighting. She gave Avery a bucket and bar of soap.

"You are lucky to be getting this kind of treatment. Most prisoners here don't get to take baths. You got a good lawyer. I still don't like you kid. You murdered all those people. I wonder why they want to give you all these luxuries." She closed the door.

Avery could hear Lucile and the guard talking from the other side. She did the best she could to clean herself. She changed into the clothes Lucile had given to her, a black and modest silk dress. It looked like something she would wear to church. Lucile also handed Avery a cup of yellow water and a toothbrush with paste smeared on it. Avery brushed her teeth. It was nice to have a makeshift shower and to be able to brush her own teeth.

"Are you done yet?" Lucile asked. She had opened the door to look at Avery. Avery felt exposed and her private space invaded.

"Yes." Lucile nodded as she saw Avery's outfit. She dried her feet on the rug outside and put on the shoes Lucile handed to her.

"Don't you look innocent?" the prison guard mocked Avery.

She doesn't know I have a crazy parasitic twin inside of me, Avery thought to herself.

"Her lawyer said she's innocent. I don't believe him. He's defending a serial killer," Lucile said. Avery did not reply. She kept her head low. Outside a parked SUV pulled up in front of the sidewalk with Lorenzo inside. It was a newer Tahoe and was black.

"So where are we going today?"

"To a clinic, the doctor's name is Dr. Barton Faulk. He will assist us with your CAT scan. After, Dr. Lisa Sen, a neurologist, will interpret the result for us."

"Are all the officers necessary?" Avery asked, glancing in the backseat.

"Yes, they will have to cuff you to the machine. Please don't put up a fight."

"I won't fight, if they aren't difficult."

The clinic was not very big. The brick was new and crème colored. The roof was made of Spanish tile. It looked very modern. Inside was a waiting room that looked like any normal doctor's office. Magazines had been spread across a glass coffee table. Dr. Faulk was waiting for them. He was a clean-cut brunette man who wore black spectacles. His blue eyes lit up when he saw Avery walk in.

"Ah, the renowned Avery Tran. Pleased to meet you." Dr. Faulk extended his hand and Avery graciously accepted.

"So, shall we get on with it?"

The group followed Dr. Faulk into the back of the clinic. The walls were grey in here as well and there was a long row of patient rooms. Barton Faulk led them to a room at the end of the hall. It was unlike what Avery thought it would be. She had envisioned something more horrifying. The room was very bright and painted a pale yellow, however. The walls had been painted with a jungle theme: monkeys, elephants, gorillas, and tigers filled the room with life, making it look quite whimsical. The CT scanner stood alone in the middle of the room. The outside of the machine was square but it had a round opening and a mechanical bed placed inside it. On the mechanical bed was thin paper. A piece of folded up cloth lay on the bed. Doctor Faulk picked it up.

"Avery would you mind putting this on?" he asked.

"Sure, that's fine. Where is the bathroom?" she replied.

"This way, Avery." Doctor Faulk showed her where the bathroom was.

"Please take off your bra. You can leave your underwear on. Thank you, Avery." One of the police officers, a female one, went into the bathroom with her.

"Is this really necessary, Lorenzo?" Avery asked.

"Yes." Avery sighed.

She closed the door and examined the clinic's gown. It was white with blue diamond shapes printed on it. It was not very comfortable and exposed her back. To make matters worse, the female police officer stared at her intently.

"Enjoying yourself?" Avery asked.

"You think I enjoy being locked in a room with a serial killer? The answer is no, but this is part of the job. I signed up to serve and protect."

"I didn't do it. My twin Venice did all of it." The officer laughed, and didn't respond. She flipped her blond ponytail in displeasure.

Finally, Avery faced her fate. She was placed on the examination table of the CT machine. The officers couldn't cuff her to the table, since Dr. Faulk complained it would distort the images.

As the CAT scanner took pictures of her body, Avery thought of her mother Muoi. She wondered who would bury her mother. Peter was too unstable to plan funeral arrangements. Anna and her husband would probably step up to the plate and do the heavy lifting. She dreaded the thought of spending life in prison, or even facing the death penalty. What she dreaded even more was the thought of going to the nail salon without her mother. All the gossiping and memories there with Muoi: it would never be the same.

After the CT scan Avery sat in one of the small patient rooms, waiting for Dr. Lisa Sen to come into the room. She was running late. There were only two police officers in the room. The rest stood outside. Lorenzo paced back and forth. He was nervous. What if Avery didn't have a parasitic twin in her? What would his argument be to the jury? He was going up against Clark Singleton. This Dallas district attorney has a ruthless reputation.

"Oh, my, I am so sorry, I am late," Lisa Sen said, opening the door. She glanced around the cramped room. She had an olive complexion and dark eyes to match her hair color.

"You guys can wait outside," Lorenzo mentioned to the officers. "She isn't going anywhere. Don't be buffoons, there are no windows. How can she escape?" he answered as one of the officers opened his mouth to protest.

"So, let's see what we have here." Lisa Sen put one of the images up on the board. She switched on the light.

"Oh, this is a horrible image. Let's use another one."

"Doctor, is it possible the parasitic twin can control Avery?" She had never heard the term parasitic twin, but now it made sense to Avery. It clicked perfectly with Venice's story about them being sisters.

"Anything is possible, I just need to get a better image." Dr. Sen adjusted her black-rimmed glasses.

"Ah, I see it now. Yes, there it is connected to her spinal

cord." She pointed to a massive cerebrum. "I didn't expect this at all. Oh, wow. It looks like it is even functioning. Just like a regular cerebrum would."

"What is a cerebrum?" Avery asked.

"A brain, dear."

"What, so Venice is a brain?"

"I believe so… the medical definition of a parasitic twin is an undeveloped twin who is completely dependent on the complete fetus called an autosite." Dr. Sen started shuffling through more images. "I can't believe it, amazing! Just fascinating, I have never seen anything like this."

"Dr. Sen, can you prove that this twin can take control of her body in court?"

"Why, certainly. I just can't believe it. This is a scientific discovery. It must be studied and recorded."

"What do you think I am? Some lab rat to be used at your disposal?" Avery was enraged by the doctor's reaction.

"Now, now, Avery. Calm yourself. Remember she is here to aid you."

"Can't you get rid of it?" Avery asked Lisa Sen.

"This is a breakthrough to science! How can I destroy it? It is beautiful! I have never encountered an unequally conjoined twin that was alive!"

"That's it! I am going to destroy her once and for all. I know where she's located now." Avery grabbed a needle off the counter. Lorenzo lunged at her and tried to restrain her.

"Guards, guards, guards!" he screamed. The police officers came busting through the door and restrained the deranged Avery. Dr. Sen injected Avery with a tranquilizer.

Avery woke up to find herself back in the filthy cell. She glanced around. She felt utterly betrayed by Lorenzo. She could have killed Venice right there on the spot. She stared at the camera.

"A needle wouldn't kill me. You could end up killing yourself," Venice said. Avery turned to see her twin.

"How's that? You're the lesser twin after all. Fully dependent on me."

"We are attached imbecile, at the spinal cord."

"Oh, I see. Venice, please go away. I am so sick of seeing you. The more I see you the more depressed I get about my situation."

"No, I am not going away."

"Why do you talk to me?" Venice strained her face. She carefully thought of her answer.

"You are my friend, we have been together since birth, and most importantly you are my twin. What more is there to say?"

"Birth, funny you say that word. It makes me think of my mother."

"Do you see how right I was about killing her? She didn't accept me, which means she didn't accept you, Avery."

"She loved me. Muoi did nothing but care for me. She got me the job at the nail salon, and she even helped pay for my books one semester for school."

"Two things, doesn't sound like much."

"You're forgetting the time Muoi broke Peter's game console."

"Look deep inside. Didn't you feel like she loved Anna more than you?"

"No, she was always raving about her."

"Yes, talking about what a good daughter she was. Don't you see that she loved Anna more than you?" Venice lowered her voice to almost a whisper. "She didn't love you because you are a freak."

"What?" Avery said, confused. She looked at her face in the reflection of a small hand mirror Lorenzo had given to her. Was it true? Did her mother love Anna more?

"Yeah, remember all the times she missed your awards ceremonies?"

"I was ten years old and in the fifth grade. I won every award except the math award." Venice smiled. Her diabolical plan was working already.

"She always showed up to that bitch Anna's award ceremonies. Never showed up to yours." Avery began to cry; she could feel herself getting weaker.

"Go to sleep, Avery. Let me take over, for a while," Venice said sweetly.

Avery slipped into a deep sleep at Venice's command.

"Yes, that's it. Good girl." Venice winked at herself in the mirror that Pennie left in Avery's cell earlier. "You are so clever aren't you?" Venice asked herself. "Now that I am in full control of Avery's body, I will escape this dreadful place."

Venice hummed quietly to herself. She enjoyed seeing the rays of the sunlight. Never before had she taken over Avery's body during the day. Avery was getting weaker and losing the ability to control her body. Venice studied the cell and thought about how to escape. The sounds of men's loafers interrupted her thoughts. A man emerged in front of the cell. He was an elderly man with grey hair and a refined aspect. His blue eyes gleamed when he saw Venice in the cell.

"Avery or Venice?"

"Ah, Dr. Neil Dean. I figured you would come. I am famous after all!" Venice said, getting up from the bed.

"So you are Venice, correct?"

"Yes, have you come to rescue me?"

"No, I came to see you."

"What do you want?"

"I just wanted to see who I was talking to."

"Are you agreeing to do the surgery?"

"You are in jail. Maybe, after the trial."

"Forget the trial. I need you now. Help me escape and I will give you riches beyond belief."

"We will see. Interesting to see you. Your picture on television is not very appealing…"

"Come here." Venice grabbed the doctor's shirt. She pulled him up to the cold bars. "Kiss me," she demanded.

"No." The doctor backed away. He left her in the cell.

"Wait, wait! Don't go! What about the surgery?" Venice screamed through the bars.

Dr. Dean thought of Venice as he drove home. He had been fascinated by her from the beginning. She had contacted him through the web and they had chatted extensively on the subject of unequally conjoined twins. Venice had told him her problem and requested surgery. The doctor's phone rang.

"Sir, the 3D printer came in the mail today."

"Excellent." The doctor smiled. Perhaps the little twin was smarter than he predicted.

Chapter Eleven

The Trial of asymmetrical twins

AVERY TWISTED AROUND IN HER COT. It was a hot night in the Dallas county jail. She couldn't sleep. The first day of the trial was tomorrow. She has been thinking of her mother quite a bit in the days leading up to it. She missed her dearly and just wanted to go home.

Meanwhile, Lorenzo sat in his office facing Pennie Apples. He was scanning over the video they had of Avery's cell. He was right to have predicted that Venice would emerge at night as Avery.

"So, now I am compiling the evidence in Avery's defense. Have you heard from Aki Hino if she will testify?"

"Well, I have contacted her, she is a difficult person to get in touch with. I think I will have to fly over to Hawaii to get in touch with her."

"What we have so far is promising. The videos clearly show Venice taking control of Avery's body in the cell. Lisa Sen has already said she will testify. We have the CT scan images on our side. I feel with the information I have, I will be able to win the jury over."

"I wonder how Avery is adjusting to all this."

"You may visit her if you wish."

"I don't know. With Venice still inside her, I don't feel safe."

"Venice has killed about five people. I see why you are fearful."

"Poor Avery, I would despise having a nuisance murderer twin inside me. It must be hard for her."

"Well, the twin is locked up with Avery. So there is not much to worry about."

"What if the jury sentences her to death by lethal injection?"

"Let's hope they don't."

"Do you know what evidence DA Singleton has?"

"Well, they have quite a bit. Avery's DNA is on the knife that was used to slit her mother's throat. Also, they have the mutilated genitals from the men and women from the swinger's club."

"How did they find that?"

"They got a search warrant for Avery's house. They were hidden under her bed."

"Tough case," Pennie said.

"I am a tough lawyer," Lorenzo responded, shuffling his paperwork.

Avery sat in the courtroom, her mind racing. The ride to the courthouse has been taxing. More protestors were lined up with their signs. They loathed Avery. The police officers were so rude to her. They made snide comments. Lorenzo was reading the summary of his opening statement. Pennie Apples sat right behind Avery. She had her notepad to record notes on the trial.

"All rise for the honorable Judge Bernice London." The judge took her place on stand. She was petite woman with hair as dark as a raven's feather. Her ancient face was creased and her aged lips were pursed.

"You may sit down," she responded. "Counselor Fernandez, please present your opening statement to the Jury."

Lorenzo walked up to the stand. He stood tall in front of the jury stand, completely confident and poised.

"Good afternoon ladies and gentlemen of the jury. You must consider Avery Tran is a twin. A pair of siblings conjoined together from birth. They share the same body." The jury gasped.

"Objection, your honor! The jury has not been presented with any evidence that the defendant is indeed a twin." The district attorney Clark Singleton was visibly upset with a face as red as tomato.

"Counselor Singleton is correct. The jury is to disregard Counselor Fernandez's last sentence."

"Ladies, and gentlemen of the jury. My name is Lorenzo Fernandez. Let me start off by saying Avery Tran is an out-standing member of the community. The unfortunate souls who were murdered were swingers. They were sinners to begin with. There is no evidence Avery was at Ninth Heaven. She is a college student, nail technician, and an overall excellent citizen. She has never committed a crime, not even getting a speeding ticket. Consider this, why would a sweet innocent Asian girl be associated with a seedy swingers club? When her whole focus in life is to be a contributing member of society! Your honor, I rest my case."

"Counselor Singleton, please present your opening state-ment." Judge London said vaguely.

"Ladies and gentlemen of the jury. My name is Clark Sin-gleton. Let me paint a picture in your head. Imagine you're a working mother of four found dead in a dumpster with her eyes and genitals mutilated. Imagine a father of two found next to the mother. His eyes are cut out and his manhood removed. We found the sex organs in a jar in Avery Tran's mother's house. According the video footage from Ninth Heaven the defendant Avery Tran was seen at 9:00pm on June 20, 2014 at this volatile establishment. She is not the little angel as Counse-lor Fernandez makes her out to be. Your honor, I rest my case."

"The prosecution may bring forth its first witness, a Mrs. Linda La Belle," the judge announced.

Linda La Belle walked into the courtroom. Avery was shocked. Of all the people she expected the prosecution to bring up. She never expected to see the exorcist. Linda La Belle appeared to look normal without her unusual garb, which she had been dressed in when performing Avery's exorcism. She still had one blue and misshapen green eye.

"Do you swear to tell nothing but the truth?" the bailiff asked her.

"I do," La Belle responded, placing her hand on the bible.

She sat down and stared around the courtroom. It was a cool day so she wrapped herself in a black wool shawl. Her stringy grey hair was tied up in a bun.

"Mrs. La Belle, can you point out and identify the defendant?" Clark Singleton began to cross examine her. She pointed to Avery. "Let the court note, Mrs. La Belle pointed and identified Avery Tran. It is true the defendant sought you out to perform the exorcism?"

"Yes, she and her friend paid me one hundred dollars to do so."

"Would you say the client has a malevolent force hidden within her?"

"No, I did not sense any of this with the girl." Avery knew she was lying and it was making her boil inside.

"Did she the defendant Avery Tran truly believe she had a demon within her controlling her?"

"No, I think she was faking it." Avery was outraged. Madame La Belle was making her seem like a lunatic.

"Do you believe Avery Tran murdered Patricia Vander, Landon Boulder, Kenneth Reed, Heather Jackson, and Muoi Tran, the defendant's own mother?"

"Yes, sir. She did it. She murdered those people!"

"Your honor, I rest my case." Clark Singleton walked back to his side of the courtroom.

"Counselor Fernandez, Are you going to be cross examining the prosecution's witness?"

"Yes, your honor."

"Proceed." The judge said.

"Mrs. La Belle, do you have any degrees or certifications for performing exorcisms?" She was caught off guard by Lorenzo's question.

"I do not, but I have performed many over the years."

"So you have no certifications to qualify you to even be an exorcist… How many exorcism have you performed?"

"I think about one hundred or so."

"How many people did you end up ripping off over the years?"

"One hundred," Mrs. La Belle answered fast. "Wait, I take

it back!" she quickly retorted.

"Your honor, I rest my case," Lorenzo said.

After a long day in court Avery was nervously pacing about in her cell. She was appalled the prosecution brought Madame La Belle into the courtroom today. The cell seemed to be shrinking by the minute. Avery was getting stir crazy: it was hard being confined and not having the freedom to do as she pleased.

"Avery, Avery, Avery how does it feel being stuck in a tiny cell?" Venice taunted from the corner of her cell.

"What do you want, secondary twin?"

"Secondary? How dare you say that to me? I am the brains behind you. I am you."

"Heh, your nothing but a squealing cerebrum who wants to be free. I am the body and I think for myself."

"Not the other day. I was able to suppress you. I am getting stronger Avery. You are getting weaker and weaker by the minute."

"No, you are, Venice. Remember you're just a brain, you don't even have a body. You would never survive without me."

"Just you wait, the jury will find you guilty and sentence you to death by electrocution!"

"You'll die too, incompetent fool!" Avery lashed back.

"Maybe I am learning how to be less dependent on you."

"How is that?"

"I will never tell you my secrets!"

"Go away, Venice. I wish you would leave!" Venice got closer to Avery. The cell's once warm glow had dimmed. Ice started forming around the bars.

"Who are you talking to?" The prison warden Lucile Black came by to check on Avery.

"Do you see the ice on the bars?" Avery asked shaking. She was freezing now.

"What ice? I don't see anything?"

"It's there." Avery touched the bars.

"What are you, insane? I see nothing. Now stop yelling or I will throw you in solidary confinement!"

Now, Avery was beginning to understand. Venice, it was

all in her head. The mind games she played with Avery earlier in her childhood. It was all in her head. No one else could see the ice forming around the bars. How powerful could her unequally conjoined twin be?

The next day was another day of court. Avery fidgeted in her seat. The courtroom was full. She waited patiently for the judge to appear. Lorenzo sat next to her wondering who the prosecution would bring to the witness stand. He knew they were going to bring in physical evidence today. Lorenzo was nervous on how he was going to defeat the prosecution. They had quite a bit on Avery. All he had going for him was a theory become reality.

"The prosecution may bring in the second witness, a Miss Phoung Dien," Bernice said after settling down in her seat.

A middle aged Vietnamese woman walked in. She was wearing a ratty blazer with an equally atrocious plaid shirt. You could tell she was far from spoon fed. Her nervous brown eyes scanned the room. Avery recognized her from the nail salon. This woman and her mother talked frequently. After swearing to tell nothing but the truth, Phoung Dien took her seat on the witness stand.

"Miss Phoung Dien, you are a friend of Muoi Tran, correct?" Clark Singleton asked.

"Yes, she is my best friend," the women answered in broken English.

"Is it true Muoi was beginning to think her daughter was becoming unhinged right before her death on April, 22, 2014?"

"Yes, sir."

"How was it Muoi's daughter Avery Tran was becoming unhinged?" The woman cleared her throat before answering.

"She said to me that Avery had been acting strange as of late."

"Strange how, Miss Dien?"

"Well, she almost burnt down the house with a stick."

"It's a smudge stick. Pennie Apples gave it to me to cleanse my room! It was supposed to aid me with the removal of Venice! My demented evil twin!" Avery screamed at the witness.

"Control your client, counselor Fernandez. Any more outbursts and I will have her removed from the courtroom," Bernice London commanded.

"Yes, your honor," Lorenzo responded. "Pipe down," he whispered to Avery.

"Miss Dien, what else did the defendant Avery Tran do to worry her mother?" Singleton continued to question the witness after the Judge's consent.

"She came home late one night wearing skimpy clothing at a very late hour. Also, she handcuffed herself to bed. Who does that? No sane person."

"Was it the day she murdered the victims?" Before the witness could answer, Lorenzo interrupted.

"Objection, your honor! There is no evidence my client Avery has committed murder."

"The jury is to disregard the last remark made by Counselor Singleton."

"No further questions, your honor."

Lorenzo cross-examined Miss Phoung Dien. He had caught on that the prosecution had rehearsed her cross-examination. He preyed on her weakest part, which was her English. How did she understand what the word unhinged meant?

The prosecution brought in a video tape of Avery's time in Ninth Heaven. She saw herself on the television and could barely control herself. She knew full well that it was Venice and not her on the retro TV.

After a long day at court, Avery crawled into her itchy cot. She thought of Phoung Dien. Avery had only had one encounter with this mysterious woman who was supposed to be her mother's best friend. She was cleaning out her station at the nail salon when Phoung approached her. She had asked her to stop worrying her mother. Avery had not thought much about it at the time. Thinking about it now, she regretted not spending more time with her mother.

The next few days of court were strenuous. The prosecution brought in the owner of Ninth Heaven. He confirmed that Avery had come to Ninth Heaven on numerous occasions.

They also brought in the jar of mutilated sex organs of the swingers. Avery puked after seeing the jar. Court was dismissed early that day. It was now Lorenzo's turn to bring up Lisa Sen.

Lisa sat in the witness stand biting her lip. She was very nervous. Her public speaking skills left much to be desired. She swallowed and took a breath. Lorenzo approached the stand.

"Doctor Sen, you were the one to interpret the photographs of the asymmetrical twin on May, 5, 2014 correct?" Lorenzo asked.

"Yes," she replied weakly.

"Can you please point to the unequally conjoined twin in the photograph?"

"Yes, it is there." She pointed at the grey object, which was the cerebrum called Venice.

"Let the court note, the witness identified the twin within the defendant Avery Tran." He showed her more photographs from the CAT scan and identified the twin in every one. Lorenzo continued: "The twin is an infectious parasite that can control Avery, can you describe how, Doctor?"

"In the first place, this twin is a cerebrum. In all my life as a neurologist, I have never encountered such a thing. You usually see asymmetrical twins as a pair of legs, an arm, and maybe a torso. Being a cerebrum and attached to Avery's spinal cord, yes, it is possible this twin is capable of controlling her. They share the same nerves, and so forth."

"I rest my case, your honor."

Lorenzo let Clark Singleton cross-examine Lisa Sen. The following day, a video of Venice controlling Avery's body was presented in court. The jury could see the difference between Venice and Avery after the video was shown. Avery was much more tame and worrisome than her twin Venice. She screamed and shouted to be released from jail. The prosecution presented more evidence to the jury of twelve. But the best was yet to come.

Chapter Twelve

Aki Hino

A VERY WAS SITTING IN A STIFF CHAIR in the courtroom staring at Aki Hino. She was a petite Japanese woman with large brown eyes. She reminded Avery of her own mother Muoi.

"Mrs. Hino, would you please tell the court why I asked you to come forward today?" Lorenzo asked her.

"I shared the same experience as Avery Tran."

"Please elaborate for the court."

"Well, about a few years ago, I almost murdered my own husband because of my unequally conjoined twin." Aki fiddled around with her floral sweater. She was nervous being in court. She was a law abiding citizen and had never before seen the inside of a courtroom.

"Please keep going," Lorenzo urged.

"That night was hot, I had gone to bed earlier than my husband. He stayed downstairs to clean up the sushi shop we own in Hawaii. I remember waking up tied up to the chair. He said I tried to kill him. He said I was not myself. We had a CAT scan conducted on my body a few days later. The doctor Neil Dean found the twin and was able to remove it. I was normal after that event."

"Is the twin still alive?"

"No."

"So you believe the twin caused you to become hostile to-wards your husband?"

"Well, what else could it be? After the twin was removed, I was free at last."

"The asymmetrical twin was also a cerebrum correct?"

"A brain connected to my spinal cord."

"Is that a yes to the question?"

"Yes, sir."

In the following days Neil Dean was brought in. He confirmed Aki Hino's experience. The prosecution was running out of witnesses and evidence. Both of the parties had strong cases. The jury of twelve deliberated. They finally came to a verdict after a few days. "Bailiff, bring in the jury," Judge London said. After the judge asked each and every juror if their verdict was unanimous and those jurors answering yes, Judge London went on to say, "Having received and agreed upon the jury's verdict, the defendant Avery Tran is not guilty by reason of insanity. The defendant's sentence will be six months in the Woodward Mental Health Facility. While incarnated in this facility, the defendant Avery Tran must undergo surgery for removal of the unequally conjoined twin to be conducted by Dr. Neil Dean. Furthermore, after removal of the twin, Miss Tran must be interviewed and tested by several of their psychiatrists in the facility in order to be released. The sentencing starts now. Court is adjourned" The judge banged the gravel and released Avery.

The courtroom was in a frenzy. Cameras flashed and reporters crammed in trying to ask Avery questions. Avery could not believe it. She sobbed: it was over, it was finally over.

"That was a fair sentence, don't you think, Avery?" Lorenzo asked.

"More than fair, finally Venice will be gone from my life forever."

Chapter Thirteen

Eternity will never separate twins

AVERY SAT IN HER NEW CELL at the Woodward Mental Health
Facility. It was much more comfortable than the cell in the Dallas County Jail. She had her own bed, no camera watching her
every move, a table full of books and magazines. Avery still
wasn't free but soon she would be without Venice. The surgery
was going to be performed tomorrow. Pennie and Lorenzo had
come by earlier to wish her well. Even the little tart Hannah
Hayes came to visit. She told Avery everything she needed to
know about her mother's funeral. Avery made sure she would
visit her mother's grave after being released from Woodward.

"Happy, happy, and even more disgustingly happy, aren't
you?" Venice said from the edge of the bed. She sat there looking glum and disappointed.

"The surgery is tomorrow. I will finally be rid of you!"
Avery said happily, kicking her feet. She knew full well she had
won the fight with Venice.

"I won't die, I will never die!"

"Oh yes, you will! Tomorrow, in fact."

"Say, it again!" Venice said, standing tall over Avery. She
shook her fists at Avery. "If only I had my way with you a long
time ago. I wouldn't be the one to die."

"Forget it Venice, your time is over." Avery was not afraid
of Venice anymore.

"My ghost will come back and haunt you!" Venice retorted.

"No, once you are gone, you are gone for eternity. There is no going back." Venice started to get very nervous. What if her agreement with Neil Dean would not work? What if he killed her like he killed Aki Hino's twin? What would happen?

"Do you believe in heaven, Avery?"

"No, but even if there was one you wouldn't get in."

"You are incorrigible!"

The next day, Avery's surgery was performed. The doctor was able to remove the twin successfully without causing harm to Avery. After a span of many hours and the assistance of a robotic arm, Avery was free from Venice. The weight from Venice's cerebrum had been lifted from her back for good.

At his home, Neil Dean carefully removed the cerebrum from his bag. He had placed it in liquid nitrogen to preserve it. The 3D printed body was just about ready for Venice. He had considered going to the morgue to get a real body, but decided against it. In the next few weeks, the doctor acted quickly. He placed Venice's cerebrum into the new body. He prayed and prayed his experiment would work. The 3D printed body started to breathe on its own. The doctor gasped, waiting for more. The wicked Venice opened her green eyes to a new world with a new body that only she could control.

An Excerpt from
"The Malevolent Twin's Retribution"

By:
Mary Sage Nguyen

Prologue

VENICE WAS IN A STATE OF LIMBO from the surgery. Limbo was fascinating. The birds flew up in the sky. It was peaceful. Venice woke up in a bed of freshly picked wildflowers. She was still in her twin's Avery body but it was different now. Avery did not inhabit this body. Only Venice did.

"Wow, this place looks feels like the Garden of Eden!" Venice shouted out loud. She scurried around with her bare feet in the soft grass. She threw handfuls of flowers, and was infatuated with the enormous developing garden around her.

"I will say, it is." She turned around to see her mother Muoi. She was dressed in a white billowing garments. A white shining halo floated above her head. She was youthful, compared to when she left the earth. Venice could only stare in awe.

"Are you, are you alive?" Venice asked. She had murdered her mother early that year.

"No, I am deceased. You murdered me remember?"

"Yes, why are you here? Where am I?"

"Come with me, wayward daughter." Venice took her mother hand. They walked for some time, she could see a waterfall at the edge of the forest.

"Are we going there?" Venice pointed to waterfall. Muoi didn't answer. They walked on, and the trees parted revealing the massive waterfall. The pair walked on the beach by the river connecting to the waterfall.

"Look at all these smooth river rocks!" Venice said excitedly, picking one up. Muoi grabbed it and threw it in the river.

"Don't grab anymore stones, not until you have decided what you want."

"What do you mean?" Venice asked.

"Venice, do you want to be saved?" Muoi asked.

"What do you mean mother?"

"Will you live the life of your dreams, if we let you return to life?"

"Am I dead?"

"If you wish."

"I don't want to die!" Venice embraced Muoi. She stroked Venice's hair.

"Will you live the life you dreamed of? Will stop the brutal punishments on innocents?"

"Will I stop murdering people?"

"Yes, and one other condition is you are not to seek vengeance on your sister Avery."

"Yes, mother. Yes, I will! I'll never stab anyone again." Venice squeezed her mother harder.

"I am glad you answered yes, now you may return to the world, you were born to."

Venice smiled with extreme pleasure. She would never be the virtuous woman, her mother wanted her to be. She would never capitulate to society. After all their regulations were meant to be broken.

ABOUT AUTHOR

Mary Sage Nguyen is the youngest daughter of Vietnamese and Chinese immigrants. Vietnamese was the language spoken at home, so the only way she was able to learn English was through the public school system. Even though English was not spoken at home, Mary became an avid reader as a young child and always dreamed of being a writer someday.

You can keep in contact with her through her website:

www.marysagenguyen.com